Innocent Ink

Inked in the Steel City Book 2

RANAE ROSE

Innocent Ink

This book is a work of fiction. All characters, names, places and events are products of the author's imagination and are in no way real. Any resemblance to real events or persons, living or dead, is entirely coincidental.

Karla,

All my BEST & HAPPY READING!

CONTENTS

CHAPTER 1

Karen walked into the Hot Ink Tattoo Studio clutching a manila envelope over her speeding heart. *Crackle.* One of the photos inside bent, and she swore softly as she pulled the envelope away from her body, desperately trying to smooth it back out. If she'd damaged the photos…

Well, if she'd damaged the photos, she'd just have to print out new ones and come back a second time. She fought a manic grin at the thought, struggling to control her expression as the door fell shut behind her, sealing out the waning heat of a summer evening in Pittsburgh.

"Hey, Karen." Mina beamed from behind the counter where a cash register rested on top of a glass display case showing off body jewelry.

"Hey." Karen's voice came out a lot less breezy than she'd intended, and for a second, a spark of amusement seemed to gleam in Mina's dark eyes.

God, was she really that obvious? There were mirrors in all five of the half-booths that lined the shop's walls, and she purposely avoided looking at any of them. Her fair skin was always quick to show a blush, and if her cheeks were as red as they felt, she didn't want to know.

"Jed's in the back," Mina called as Karen made her way down the aisle between booths.

"I figured," Karen said, cringing inwardly. If she hadn't looked ridiculously excited to see him when she'd walked in with flaming cheeks and a goofy smile, she'd ruined that by making a beeline toward the back of the shop without waiting for Mina to direct her. She'd just been so eager to escape Mina's knowing gaze – sometimes, having a best friend who worked at the place her crush owned did *not* seem like an advantage.

Crackle. The envelope protested again as she raised a fist to knock on the closed door Jed was definitely behind. She couldn't help being aware of her heartbeat – it was pounding so loudly in her ears that it almost drowned out the not-so-distant buzzing of a tattoo machine – as her knuckles hit wood.

"Come on in." Jed's voice was so deep that it reverberated somewhere in her core – a place she tried hard not to think about as she turned the doorknob and stepped into the combined office and storage space Jed sometimes worked in when he wasn't tattooing or consulting with a client.

"Karen." Jed looked up from the desk that took up one corner, his dark eyes a little wider than usual as he placed large hands on its surface and rose.

He looked surprised, which wasn't exactly shocking – she'd sent him an e-mail telling him she was headed to Hot Ink, but that had been a whopping twenty minutes ago, and she'd high-tailed it to the studio, unable to resist the lure of showing him her latest work in person. She'd more or less memorized his work hours – a completely natural result of having done so much work for his business, of course.

As she stood before his desk, her gaze was drawn to him like a magnet to iron.

He was tall. About 6'3" if Karen's estimation was correct, and she was a pretty good judge of height – a consequence of being a 5'10" tall woman. Some guys were shorter than her, and most weren't much taller. But Jed … she noticed every last one of the several inches in their height difference, and his muscular frame made him seem even bigger.

"I brought you those photos." She lifted the manila envelope and held it between them like it could shield her from the sexiness that radiated from the owner of the Hot Ink Tattoo Studio. The photos were feeble protection against his short but not too-short, almost-black hair and the dark stubble that shadowed his jaw. His dark eyes met hers, and she stood frozen. Some idiotic nervous instinct urged her to hop back and forth, or at least shift her weight from foot to foot, but she stifled the urge.

"McGinnis' back piece?" Jed rounded the desk and practically pried the envelope from her suddenly stiff fingers.

He took it from her, and with a crackle and a flash of script, it was in his hands. *Jed Torino* – she'd written his name across the envelope, as if she could possibly forget who it was meant for. It had taken all her willpower not to dot the 'I' in Torino with a heart, or to scrawl her own name next to it.

"Yeah," she said breathlessly. "I finished going through the images a little early last night, and there were some that turned out so well I couldn't resist making prints. And well, I thought you might like to look at them in person instead of on a computer screen."

"This is great," Jed said, sliding the stack of prints out of the envelope. "I was only expecting an e-mail, but this is even better."

"Hope you like them." Her voice came out higher than it should have, sort of like she'd just inhaled a lungful of helium. Her face warmed, but luckily, Jed had his head bent over the photos, which he shuffled through slowly, holding the prints gingerly between large fingers, studying each one.

Karen's heart thumped against her ribs like an unhappily-confined animal against steel bars. This was exactly the reason why she'd come to the studio in person. When Jed looked at her work, it was like he was in his own little world – a world that revolved around his passion and hers, which were tattooing and photography, respectively. He handled the amazing ink work and she photographed it in the most flattering way she knew how; in a way, it was like they worked together to create something beautiful.

Maybe the thought was a little cheesy, but she liked – no, loved – anything that involved her and Jed collaborating

"These are amazing." Jed carefully slipped a photo to the bottom of the stack, raising his gaze briefly to meet her eyes before poring over the next one. "As usual."

"Thank you." She resisted the urge to fan herself with the empty envelope as she studied him studying her work. With the exception of his ridiculously handsome face and his neck, Jed was covered in tattoos. There was even ink on his hands, dark and vibrant over the bulges of bones and sinew beneath the surface. It all added to his appeal. He was tall, dark and handsome in a bad-boy sort of way that made her head spin so fast she tripped a little and bumped her thigh on the corner of the nearby desk.

"You okay?" Jed asked, abandoning his perusal of the photos and shooting her a look full of concern.

"Fine," she breathed, resisting the urge to search for a nearby rock to hide under. Most people didn't trip while standing still. She was not most people.

She was so accident prone that she'd actually invented a few vivid fantasies that involved her tripping and Jed conveniently scooping her up, her knight in tattooed armor to the rescue... Thinking about those daydreams while standing right in front of him made her wish she could wipe her brain's memory clean just in case Jed developed the ability to read minds.

"Are these the final images?" Jed asked, holding one aloft.

"Yes. I mean, unless there's something you don't like about them? I could always pop them into Photoshop and—"

"No," he interrupted, "they're perfect. It's just that you're usually so adamant about editing images before you'll let me use them. I can never find anything I don't like about them, but I've gotten to know you well enough to realize that your standards are higher than mine." He grinned at her in a way he probably thought was good-natured. In reality, it made her feel in danger of melting from the inside out.

"I've already put those images through the editing process. Your client has great skin – I didn't have to touch up much. I just brightened the colors and cleaned up the background a little." Jed kept looking at her, and she knew she'd said all that needed to be said, but the words just kept coming. "Hardly any work at all, really, and *voilà*, they're ready to go."

Voilà?

She was naturally chatty and she knew it, but when she was around Jed, sometimes she spoke just because the idea of silence made her nervous. Afterward, she almost always regretted it.

He still held her gaze captive. His eyes were so dark that his gaze always seemed intense when he turned it on her directly. "They look great. Thanks again for photographing McGuiness for me. I'm going to add these images to my online portfolio and the studio's main page as soon as I get them in an e-mail from you."

"Great. But it wasn't hard to photograph, really – you did such an amazing job with that tattoo that it was easy to take a flattering picture." The back piece Jed had done for McGinnis featured a ship sailing at full mast, riding waves that reflected the vibrant colors of a setting sun. It was amazing – so amazing she could almost see the waves moving and the sunlight shining on the water's choppy surface when she looked at the pictures.

"Thanks." He held her gaze for another moment before finally lowering his eyes and sliding the photos back into the envelope. "Do you need these back?"

"No, you can keep them. I can always print out more if I need them."

"Thanks."

"Yeah." Her excuse for lingering in Jed's office had evaporated like a drop of water in a hot frying pan, but her legs didn't listen when she willed them to move. "So uh, just let me know whenever you have another spectacular project you want me to photograph, okay?"

She didn't have any other sessions lined up for Hot Ink at the time, but she'd already photographed well over a dozen Hot Ink clients, plus the photo shoot with Mina and Eric that had started it all. Jed had been using some of the photographs in advertisements for the studio and on its website. Sometimes, when one of his clients had an especially unique or elaborate tattoo done, Jed offered them a Hot Ink gift certificate and free photo prints in exchange for posing for Karen.

The shoots were easy and fun – the unique and beautiful ink Jed gave his clients kept things fresh, made sure Karen had something different to photograph each time. And best of all, doing semi-frequent photo sessions on behalf of the studio meant she was often in contact with Jed – via e-mail, phone and all the in-person visits she could muster up some semblance of an excuse to make.

"I will," he said, nodding. "Got a client coming in in a couple weeks for another back piece. If it turns out like I think it will, I'd love to have some professional shots of it for my portfolio."

"No problem." The soft lash of her own ponytail against the back of her neck alerted her to the fact that she was nodding too eagerly. Purposely stilling her bobbing head, she looked directly into Jed's eyes. "Just let me know when the tattoo's ready to be photographed – I can always find room in my schedule for Hot Ink clients." After all, the first photo shoot she'd done for Hot Ink six months ago had been what had really launched her full-time photography career.

"About that," Jed said, frowning. "I know your schedule has really picked up lately. I feel bad about taking up so much of your time when you're so in demand."

"Don't worry about it." Karen didn't even try to restrain her movements as she shook her head, the end of her ponytail whipping her jaw. "The tattoo shoots don't take long, honestly. I go into the shoot knowing exactly what I want to focus on, and I've picked up some tips and tricks on how to showcase tattoos."

"At least let me pay you more. I know you're shooting for Hot Ink at a much lower rate than you charge your other clients – I looked at your website."

Karen's heart did a funny little flip-flop maneuver at the thought of Jed browsing her website, taking in all the little details of her work – sort of like how she browsed Hot Ink's website, frequently stopping by Jed's personal page to stare at his portrait.

"No way. The rate stays as it is. I owe you a lot, Jed – that photo shoot I did for Hot Ink's display windows and ads got me a lot of attention and gave me the confidence to quit waitressing and pursue my photography full-time. I'd still be hefting around platters of ribs and beer and waiting for a big break if it wasn't for you."

Jed smiled, flashing a half-grin that showed a little tooth and nearly stopped Karen's heart. "You're too kind. I feel like I'm taking advantage of you."

"You're not – I've actually been earning more since quitting my old job. I'm fine." The admission sparked an internal glow. She *was* making more money as a full-time photographer than she'd been making as a full-time waitress and part-time photographer. That had been the case for months, but when she really thought about it, it still seemed a little surreal.

Jed shook his head. "I'll wear you down eventually. Until then ... thanks." He waved the envelope. "I really appreciate the photos. Did Mina tell you how much our business has increased since we launched those ads and added some of your photography to our artists' portfolios?"

Karen grinned. "She mentioned it."

Something vibrated in the vicinity of Karen's left butt cheek, and she jumped.

Jed's dark brows rose an inch or two. "You okay?"

"Just my phone," she mumbled, pulling the object in question out of her back pocket. She swiped her thumb across the screen, keeping her head bowed – maybe reading the text she'd just received would buy her enough time to lose the blush that had burned its way across the bridge of her nose.

Just took some pumpkin pie out of the oven. Want to stop by for dinner? We can order in from that noodle place you like.

Karen read the text a second time, her gaze slowing over the glorious words 'pumpkin pie' and 'noodle place'. Nothing compared to her grandmother's pumpkin pie, but the soba noodles from her favorite Japanese restaurant were a distant second – and that was saying something.

"Everything okay?" Jed asked.

Karen shut her mouth as subtly as possible, cringing inwardly as the fact that she'd just licked her lips registered. "Yeah, that was just a dinner invitation."

"A date?"

"No." The fact that he thought she'd been licking her lips at the mere thought of a date caused her to die a little inside. "It was from my grandmother."

He grinned again for some reason. "I won't keep you, then."

"Okay. See you around, Jed."

She turned without tripping, stumbling or licking her lips and made a relatively cool exit, passing the door and emerging into the aisle between the artists' half-booths. She strode down it, ignoring the butterflies that burst into flight inside her stomach at the buzzing sound of a tattoo in progress. Yes, she loved photographing tattoos, but watching one be done usually made her feel faintly queasy. Needles ... ugh. She clutched her phone a little too tightly and typed a reply to her grandmother, Helen.

Be there in twenty. :)

"See ya, Mina." Tucking her phone back into her pocket, she paused at the front desk. It wasn't like she could leave without saying goodbye to her best friend, even if Mina *was* wearing an infuriatingly knowing little smile. It was easy for her to laugh at someone else getting flustered – she was already engaged to Eric, the artist who sat in the nearest half-booth and was responsible for the current buzzing sound.

With his dark hair and blue eyes, Eric was gorgeous, and perfect for Mina, but he didn't hold a candle to Jed. Jed was taller, darker ... more rugged. She forced herself to make eye contact with Mina, refusing to glance toward the back of the shop.

"What'd Jed think of the photos?" Mina asked, leaning on the glass display case full of body jewelry. Was it only a trick of the evening light, or did she actually waggle her eyebrows up and down a little bit?

"He loved them."

"As usual." Mina smiled and tipped her head, sending her dark, straight hair swinging.

"Yeah, well, it was the back piece he did for that McGuiness guy. The one with the sailing ship? It's an amazing tattoo."

"Mmmhmm." Mina just kept smiling, looking like the cat that had eaten the canary.

For the millionth time, Karen wished for the ability to travel back in time and stop herself on the night she'd split a bottle of champagne with Mina – to celebrate becoming a full-time photographer – and confessed how hot she thought Jed was. Just the thought of it was enough to turn her cheeks red; she'd actually used the words 'tall, dark and handsome' to describe him out loud.

"What's *mmmhmm* supposed to mean?" she whispered, just in case any of the other artists or clients were listening in.

"It's just that he always loves your photos. He loves everything you do."

Karen gave Mina her fiercest *for-the-love-of-God-speak-quietly* stare.

Mina just grinned. It was official – she was exacting revenge upon Karen for pushing her and Eric together. And she *had* literally pushed Mina out of her hiding place in a restaurant bathroom once, when Mina had been having doubts about whether Eric was really attracted to her.

Karen preferred to think that she'd assisted in boosting Mina's confidence. And it had all worked out in the end – Mina and Eric were engaged now. Very happily engaged.

"Guess I'll see you Friday," Karen said, choosing to ignore Mina's waggle-browed smile and teasing comments.

"Of course you will." Mina straightened, placing her hands flat on the countertop. "We'll all be there – me, Eric, Jess and Jed."

Karen's heart stopped, then banged back to life again. "Jed?" Why in the world would Jed be at Ruby's on Friday night? Had Mina actually invited him? Had he actually agreed to come?

"Didn't anyone tell you? You two share the same birthday."

"Who would tell me besides you?" Karen whisper-yelled, looking right into her friend's eyes.

Mina grinned. "Eric just told me yesterday. We figured we could all celebrate together. Abby, James and Tyler are coming too."

Abby, James and Tyler were Hot Ink's other tattoo artists, and the fact that they'd be attending would make Jed's presence seem more natural. Not that Karen's shameless imagination wasn't already perfectly convinced that Jed's presence would make the night nothing short of magical. Amazingly, awkwardly magical, considering the fact that Mina would probably be waggling her eyebrows and scheming to embarrass Karen at some point. Where had her sweet, reserved friend gone?

Engagement had changed her. Before she'd placed the order for her Tattooed Prince Charming's wedding tux, she'd never waggled her eyebrows at anyone.

"See you then," Karen said, stepping away from the counter.

Mina smiled. "Bye, Karen."

* * * * *

Black was a good color. You couldn't go wrong with black, right? Jed shoved his shirtsleeves up to his elbows and rolled them so they'd stay in place. He hated when sleeves touched his wrists, so he'd compromised. Usually, he wore a t-shirt, but for tonight, he'd chosen a shirt that actually buttoned up the front.

Because it was Karen's birthday. It was his birthday too, but that didn't matter. He glanced at the rearview mirror and made sure there wasn't anything on his face, like a giant sign reading *I wore sleeves for Karen because I think she's amazing.*

Nothing. He grimaced at his reflection and looked away, opening the door.

What the hell was wrong with him? Karen was too innocent, too young, too ambitious – too *everything* – for someone like him, and he hadn't been interested in a relationship in years. How old was she turning anyway? He mulled the possibilities over as he exited his Charger, gripping a box he'd wrapped just hours ago.

Ruby's, Karen's former place of employment, was packed on a Friday night. The interior was loud, and a little dark. Even over the noise of dozens of diners, he was able to pick out Karen's voice. "You have to try the strawberry lemonade, Abby," she said from a corner table.

"Of course it's alcoholic. And don't worry – we won't get stiffed on drinks here. Nate's working the bar tonight, and he makes them strong."

Jed arrived at the table just in time to see Karen winking at Abby.

Good God, she looked amazing. Not Abby – Karen. Abby might've looked good too, but Karen stole the spotlight so completely that there was no telling. Her blue-green dress stood in alluring contrast to her dark red hair and creamy skin, plenty of which was exposed by the low V-neck. She was leaning toward Abby, jabbing a finger enthusiastically at the drink menu, and the position showcased her ample cleavage like a dream.

"Jed!" Eric called out from one end of the table, where he sat with his arm around Mina. "Happy birthday, man."

His words unleashed a floodgate. The entire table erupted in a chorus of well-wishes, drowning out the rest of the noise completely for a few seconds. The outburst took him by surprise; when he'd laid eyes on Karen, he'd forgotten that it was his birthday, too.

He strode toward the table, acknowledging their sentiments with a nod, and took the nearest empty seat. It just so happened to be the seat directly across from Karen.

Tyler elbowed Jed in the side. "Already ordered a pitcher of your favorite."

"Thanks." Jed's mouth went momentarily dry as he stared across the table, and not just because Tyler's statement had him craving beer. Maybe he shouldn't have taken the seat across from Karen – he couldn't help staring at her in that dress. He had to look like an idiot. He *felt* like an idiot.

A rush of hot air and a sizzle came from behind, and a waitress spared him by lowering a platter of battered, spicy-smelling shrimp onto the table in front of him. It was an appetizer platter big enough for the entire group, and she'd barely placed a couple bowls of dipping sauce on the table top before everyone began reaching for the food.

Jed grabbed one of the shrimp and dipped it blindly into a sauce bowl, forcing himself to look at everyone seated around the table as he chewed, not just Karen.

Tyler, James, Abby and Eric – all Hot Ink's artists were there, plus Mina, one of the studio's receptionists and Eric's fiancée. Mina's little sister Jess was there too, eating shrimp and smiling as she sat in her wheelchair beside a teenaged boy who had to be her boyfriend. The kid was grinning at Jess with a distinctly dopey, instantly recognizable young love kind of look.

The sight of the two kids smiling at each other and goofing off with a couple of severed shrimp tails sent a pang of searing nostalgia through Jed's chest. His heart beat slowly but deliberately beneath the buttoned-up front of his shirt, reminding him that it was still stubbornly functioning even after being broken.

He understood the all-or-nothing nature of young love; the memory of it shimmered across the surface of his mind, startlingly vivid for a few fleeting seconds.

He shoved the memories away. He was in the middle of celebrating his thirty-fifth birthday, for fuck's sake. There was no ring on his finger, though the band he'd once worn had left a permanent mark against his skin, fainter than a tattoo, but just as lasting. This was where the love that had once consumed him had left him.

CHAPTER 2

"It was a disaster," Abby said, shaking her head, still in conversation with Karen. "Wasn't it, Jed?" She turned blue eyes on Jed, snapping him out of his self-pity with her unexpected question.

"Disaster?"

"The cover-up job I finished today. The original tattoo was a disaster, wasn't it?"

Jed grimaced. "That's putting it kindly. It was a fucking travesty." Remembering himself, he glanced toward the kids at the end of the table. Luckily, they were too absorbed in each other's company to spare any attention for what he was saying.

Abby grinned, and Karen frowned. "See, that's another thing that scares me about tattoos – there are so many horrible ones out there. What if you went to get something beautiful and it turned out to be an embarrassment?"

"A legitimate artist would make sure you got something that made you happy." Jed's gaze was drawn to the creamy skin of Karen's chest and arms. An unblemished, unmarked canvas – her skin was perfect, and so fair that ink of any color would contrast brilliantly. If she ever decided to be tattooed … what wouldn't he give to be the one to put the ink in her skin? "And they'd never even consider putting something as pathetic as the trash Abby covered up on someone's body."

"*Never*," Abby said, raising her eyebrows as she turned wide blue eyes on Karen. "The scratcher who did the original tattoo should be thrown in prison, if you ask me."

Jed's lips threatened to quirk into a smile. Abby was generally quiet, but she had her convictions.

"If I ever got a tattoo, I know where I'd go," Karen said. "Not that I want anyone to come near me with a needle, but if I did…" She met Jed's gaze for a moment so brief he would've doubted it had happened if it hadn't been for the electricity it sent crackling through his entire body.

Her gaze flickered downward just as the waitress arrived with what looked like the lemonade Karen had been talking about.

Karen gripped her glass, long fingers curling gracefully around the frosted surface, and raised it to her mouth. The plastic straw drifted through a sea of ice to part her lips, and Jed had to look away.

For the better part of an hour, he pretended to be deeply interested in the jokes, beer and food circulating around the table. After way too many shrimp, he devoured the ribs he'd ordered, and they were good, but it was hard to focus on anything when Karen's presence drove him to constant distraction. The way her hair shone in the low lighting, the way her skin glowed – everything about her drew his eye, and it was hell trying to resist.

He was on his way back from a trip to the restroom when he ran into her – not quite literally, but almost – in the narrow hallway that led to the men's and ladies' rooms.

"Oh!" Her strappy sandals slid a little on the tile, but she steadied herself with a hand against the wall just as he reached for her.

His hand swept through empty air – she'd already regained balance. He lowered it, his fingertips tingling with unfulfilled expectation. "Sorry."

"It's okay." She looked a little flushed – her fair skin was distinctly pink across her cheeks and the bridge of her nose, and her eyes were bright. If that was the effect the lemonade was having on her, he might just have to buy her a second one … as a friendly treat to the birthday girl, of course, nothing more.

"I've always thought this hall was way too narrow. Drove me crazy when I was working here." She straightened the front of her dress, and for the first time, he noticed the sequins glittering at the hem. Blue and green, they highlighted the pale but healthy sheen of her skin.

"Guess I take up more room than the average customer," he said, jerking his gaze up and trying to sound jovial. It was no joke, though – he'd barely have to raise his arms at all to touch both walls. He was used to spaces seeming cramped; it was an everyday thing, thanks to the fact that he was 6'3".

"That makes two of us," Karen said, tucking a strand of auburn hair behind one ear and looking down as she smiled, her lower lip dented where she was clearly biting it from the inside.

"What are you talking about?" Even in her strappy heeled sandals, she wasn't tall enough to look him in the eye. But she was tall enough that he didn't feel like he was talking to his toes when he looked down at her, and that was nice.

The dent in her lower lip grew deeper, wider. "Well, you know." She waved a hand at nothing. "I'm pretty tall, if you haven't noticed."

Oh, he'd noticed everything about her, including her mile-long legs, which accounted for her above-average height. "You're still short in my book," he teased.

Most people were. If Karen took up more room in the hallway than the average woman, it was less because of her height and more because of her amazing curves, which dominated the space between them and his imagination alike. She was curvy, but her waist was noticeably smaller than her hips and bust ... she was like a pin-up girl from decades past, a retro-styled tattoo come to life.

The thought called his dick to attention as she stared at him, her green eyes wide above flushed cheeks and glossed lips. He was semi-hard, and fighting a full-fledged erection with everything he had because he had to walk back to the table. And damn it, there were *kids* back at the table, not to mention almost every single one of his employees.

"Sorry," he said again, and tore his gaze away from her face, "about almost knocking you over."

"It's all right."

The hallway really was narrow. They were standing so close he could smell her perfume – a light citrusy scent that reminded him of her youth. "I won't keep you any longer." He eased past her – a serious feat, considering the hall's scant width and the fact that a part of him actually *wanted* to brush up against her – and strode toward the other side of the restaurant.

With his belly pressed to the bar, the state of arousal his encounter with Karen had left him in was well-hidden. He lingered, and when the bartender looked his way, he ordered a shot of bourbon over ice. The cold liquor burnt smooth and fiery on the back of his tongue, both heating and cooling him from the inside. He drained the glass, willing the potent fumes to erase the memory of Karen's perfume from his consciousness.

It didn't work. The airy, fruity scent lingered in his nostrils – how was it possible that he could still smell her? Half hopefully and half guiltily, he glanced toward the corridor that led to the restrooms. He could already imagine how she'd look emerging from the hall – pretty, perfect and way out of his league.

* * * * *

Karen fought the instinctive urge to turn and face Jed as he approached the table and sank back down in his chair. Where had he been? She was so hyper-aware of his presence – or lack thereof – that she noticed when he was gone. He hadn't been at the table when she'd returned a few minutes ago.

Tyler elbowed Jed, grinning. "Beer not good enough for ya?"

What did that mean?

Jed smiled a smile that didn't quite reach his eyes and shook his head.

"Lay off him," James said. "It's his birthday. Matter of fact, I think we should order a round of shots for the whole table."

Jed frowned. "There are kids here. Take it easy."

"Easy for you to say," James muttered. "Are we taking turns sneaking to the bar?"

Karen eyed the bar at the other side of the restaurant. If Jed had stopped by for a drink, she couldn't blame him – not when she was already craving another one in the wake of the lemonade cocktail she'd recently finished. Being around Jed put her nerves on edge in a bittersweet way, and it would be nice to have something to take the edge off. Then again...

She'd blurted out her crush-confession to Mina after having half a bottle of champagne. Maybe she should resist the urge to soak her nerves in alcohol – who knew what she'd say to Jed's face if she overindulged.

"You were right about the lemonade," Abby said, rattling the ice left in the bottom of her drained glass. "It's amazing. Should I ask the waitress for two more?"

"Uh..." Well, she could always sip her next drink slowly. Very slowly.

But she didn't. The straw was making slurping sounds as she pushed it to the very bottom of the ice by the time Mina stood up at one end of the table and announced that she had a gift for Karen.

"You really didn't have to," Karen said, accepting the beautifully wrapped box Mina handed her.

"Of course I did," Mina replied with a smile.

Karen untied an artfully-curled white ribbon and tore the golden wrapping paper, revealing a plain white box. When she lifted the lid, something green-grey peeked from beneath layers of tissue paper. It was soft between her fingertips as she lifted it from the box.

"Wow, Mina, this is beautiful." It was a summertime sweater – an airy knit with short flutter sleeves, done in tones of dove grey, moss green and steely blue.

"I thought it would really bring out your eyes," Mina said with a smile.

Karen gently lowered the sweater back into the box. Mina understood her style exactly. "I love it. Thanks."

"You're welcome. Happy twenty-fifth birthday."

Abby said something about how the sweater would complement Karen's hair, and Karen nodded, thanking her too as she reached automatically for her glass. Condensation cooled her fingers, at odds with the heat she could feel, the pressure of someone's gaze.

Not just anyone's gaze – Jed's gaze. She could feel it. It shouldn't have mattered – everyone had watched her open the gift, after all. But she couldn't help noticing.

"Hey Jed, we've got a gift for you too," Tyler announced, alleviating the silence.

Mina watched as Tyler waved an arm, grinning.

As if on cue, the waitress appeared, carrying a tray laden with shot glasses.

"I hereby declare that *everyone* must take a shot in honor of the birthday boy," Tyler announced. He shot a quick sideways glance at Jess and her boyfriend, Blake. "Everyone of age, I mean."

Jess and Blake were so lost in their own little world that they hardly seemed to notice the waitress lowering the glasses onto the table. Ah, young love. Karen couldn't help but smile when she looked at the two of them. They'd been seeing each other ever since they'd attended the homecoming dance together months ago, and they were adorable.

"Hold on," Jed said.

Karen raised her gaze, daring to look at him directly for the first time since she'd returned from the restroom. Was he really serious about not drinking in front of the kids – could he be about to send the drinks back?

For someone who looked like sin in rolled-up shirtsleeves, he was surprisingly conservative.

But he didn't say anything to the waitress. Instead, he looked directly into Karen's eyes. "I have a gift for Karen, too."

Karen's heart launched itself into a series of cartwheels. He had a gift for her? Seriously?

He reached under his chair and retrieved a giftwrapped box a third of the size of the one Mina had given her. It was wrapped too, in teal paper, no ribbon. She willed her hand to stay steady as she reached across the table, accepting it.

Jed's fingertips brushed hers, sparking an electric sensation that raced throughout her entire body. "Thanks. You really didn't have to get me anything. I…" She hadn't gotten him a gift. She hadn't dared, even after she'd discovered that he shared her birthday.

She broke eye contact, staring intently at the gift instead as she peeled back the wrapping paper. Even it was masculine – the deep blue-green color suited Jed. Heck, the same color was visible on his skin, in some places – all sorts of colors were, thanks to his tattoos.

After divesting the box of its wrappings, she lifted its lid, revealing something blue. A soft shade of blue – a lot like the blue in her new sweater, actually – with golden embellishments.

It was a camera strap. She lifted it, unfolded it and ran it through her fingers. It was sturdy but beautiful, definitely not cheap. She'd admired some like it online just the week before, but hadn't been able to bring herself to shell out the cash. A little tag near one end confirmed that it was the trendy brand she'd been lusting after. The little golden fleur-de-lis designs that had been embroidered onto the strap looked even better in person than they had online.

"Wow, Jed. This is beautiful. I'll definitely use it."

Every. Single. Day. She'd use it even if she didn't need it, and not just because it was so pretty.

"But you know, you really didn't have to get me anything. Now I feel bad that I didn't get you a gift."

He shrugged, his broad shoulders straining the dark fabric of his ridiculously sexy shirt. "Don't worry about it. I wanted to get you something – you've done so much for Hot Ink. You deserve a gift." He motioned toward the camera strap. "You deserve a lot more than that, actually, but I saw it in a camera shop and thought it would look nice on you."

Her cheeks burst into figurative flame as he held her gaze, eyes dark and more intense than his casual shrug.

"Thank you." For once, she didn't ramble or babble. No other words came as she lowered the strap back into its box, carefully replacing the tissue paper.

Time flew after that – each moment Karen spent trying not to stare at Jed seemed to take forever, but when she slipped up and caught his eye, the evening seemed to melt away in fleeting hours instead of minutes.

Eventually Mina and Eric rose to leave, along with Jess and Blake, saying something about the kids having some sort of extracurricular weekend trip related to their school's art club starting the next morning.

Karen nodded, smiled, hugged Mina and thanked her again for the sweater, butterflies fluttering in the pit of her stomach all the while. Jed wasn't making any move to leave, and neither were the others from Hot Ink. In fact, they'd just ordered another round of drinks.

"Have a great rest of the night," Mina whispered in Karen's ear, leaning back with the tiniest of winks.

"You've gotten downright evil lately, you know that?" Karen whispered back, careful to keep her voice low. "I can't believe you're leaving me."

"Eric and I both volunteered to chaperone the art club's summertime weekend trip, and that means getting up at five tomorrow morning. Obviously, the others aren't ready to call it a night yet. You'll have fun without us — you're among friends."

"They're your co-workers, not mine. I don't know any of the others half as well as I know Jed."

Mina's smile broadened. "So talk to Jed. See you, Karen. I'll give you a call and let you know how the trip goes."

"You do that," Karen said, fighting a fit of nervous laughter as she watched her friend leave, waving until she could no longer do so without looking like a weirdo.

Cheeks still blazing, she finally turned around.

"For the birthday girl." Abby pressed a shot glass into Karen's hand.

"What is it?" Karen asked, staring down into the shallow depths of the shot glass. A furtive glance around the table revealed several sets of hands clutching the little cups, all of them full of the same greenish mixture.

"It's a kamikaze. You'll like it. Come on!" She thrust a hand into the air, raising her own glass.

Karen shot a sideways glance at the empty glasses crowding the space in front of her and Abby and noticed for the first time that Abby had already knocked back several of the potent lemonades Nate the bartender considered his specialty.

Karen had been too busy worrying about Jed to notice. Fortunately, she'd also been too busy to order another drink. She'd had two lemonades, but the first had been almost two hours ago, and she'd had a big meal. She could afford to have a shot with the group. Maybe it would do her good – Jed's gift had sharpened the edge on her nerves considerably.

She drained her shot glass along with the others, on Abby's count.

It wasn't bad. Her lips burned a little in the wake of it, and she focused on the sensation as she paid way too much attention to her empty glass.

"What'd you think?" Abby's glass clinked loudly against the table top as she set it down.

"Not bad," Karen said, looking up to smile at Abby and catching Jed's eye.

"We should do another round!" Abby declared, and Tyler agreed, high-fiving her.

Oh, boy. The Hot Ink staff seemed a lot rowdier after dark and away from the studio than they did at work. Was this how they released the tension of having to concentrate so intently on their art all day? All of them except Jed … he was still sitting calmly, and was probably the only other person at the table besides Karen whose head wasn't spinning.

He smiled a faint half-smile. "You look a little flushed. You don't have to let Abby ply you with shots if you don't want to."

Karen laughed as Abby whirled around from her conversation with Tyler, her expression indignant. "Of course she wants to. It's her birthday! And it's yours too, Jed. When are you going to lighten up?"

Jed just smiled and shook his head. "Someone has to open up the shop tomorrow."

Abby groaned. "Holy crap, Jed. James can handle that for once! Live a little."

James, who was halfway through what looked like one of Nate's lethal Long Island Iced Teas, looked utterly hapless.

The next hour sped by in a blur of shots and cocktails, most of which were imbibed by Abby, Tyler and James. Karen took a tentative sip of a lemonade Abby had ordered for her, then left it barely-touched when she glanced at her phone and saw that it was approaching midnight.

"I'm going to get going, guys." Her grandmother was taking her to a birthday brunch at her favorite winery, not far from the city, the next morning. The last thing she wanted was to show up red-eyed and drowsy.

"I should head out too," Jed said, flattening his hands on the table and pushing back his chair. "I don't think I trust any of you three to open up shop tomorrow, and I've got a session scheduled for noon, anyway. I'll leave cash for my bill – make sure the waitress gets it, and tell her to keep the change."

"Nooo!" Abby cried when Jed pulled out his wallet. "No way. Don't you dare leave any money! This is on us."

James echoed her, and Tyler went so far as to give Jed a shove. "Get out of here. You're not paying for anything tonight."

Jed didn't move – Tyler's shove might as well have been a spring breeze. He did slip his wallet back into his pocket, though.

"You too, Karen," Abby said. "Your money's no good here." She wagged a finger and managed to look stern for about half a second.

"Thanks a lot, guys." Karen gripped her purse strap. It was a good thing the prospect of walking outside the restaurant with Jed had her so nervous she wasn't capable of laughter.

"I never realized Abby was so … lively," Karen said as she and Jed walked away from the table together. "She's always so into her work at the shop, I hardly ever hear a word out of her."

"She's not always like this. Abby's got a hot and cold personality – when she's quiet, she's quiet, and when she's not, she's really not."

Karen gripped her purse strap, thinking of the camera strap she'd tucked inside. "It was nice of them to cover our checks." The other artists had bought Jed dinner and drinks. Should she pick up a belated birthday gift for him, or would that be weird?

"Yeah. Hey, do you need a ride home?"

"I was going to call a cab," she said, pausing by the door and gripping her purse strap even harder. "You're not going to drive, are you?" Her heart plummeted down to her toes at the thought. Jed, drive after drinking? It went against everything she'd thought she'd known about him.

"I am."

"I don't think..." She mustered up all of her courage and looked him dead in the eye. "I realize I'm a lot smaller than you Jed, but if you try to get behind the wheel, I'm going to have to find a way to stop you." Maybe she could lasso him with the fancy camera strap he'd given her or something. The thought was daunting, but what other choice would she have?

Years ago, Mina and Jess had both been injured in a car accident because their mother had driven under the influence of drugs. And now Jess couldn't walk.

When Jed laughed, anger rose up inside Karen, sharp and hot. "Don't laugh. I'm serious."

"I know you are – I can see it in your eyes. I didn't have any of those shots Abby and Tyler ordered, Karen. That fruity crap doesn't sit well with me. I did drink a little, but that was hours ago, and I'm sober as a judge, I promise."

Karen's cheeks began to heat as she mentally tallied the alcohol he'd consumed during their long hours at Ruby's. She'd seen him drink a beer with his meal, and then he'd had whatever drink he'd ordered at the bar a couple hours ago. Was that really it? Two drinks, with a big meal, over the course of several hours, for a man approximately the size of a bull... "Sorry. I didn't realize..."

"It's okay. I tried not to let Abby notice I wasn't drinking those kamikaze things she loves so much, so if no one caught on, I'm in the clear. Well, no one except Tyler – he drank mine, but he won't tell."

Karen couldn't resist a bubble of nervous laughter. "I feel like such an idiot. I guess I'm the one who had a little too much to drink – I just assumed you were joining in." She hadn't gone wild, but a light buzz blurred the edges of her thoughts and amplified her emotions.

"Don't worry about it. Can I give you that ride? I hate to think of you riding alone in the backseat of a cab on your birthday."

"Okay." It wasn't like she savored the idea of a cab ride either, especially compared to the allure of being chauffeured by a shirt-sleeves wearing, sexy-as-sin Jed. Technically, her apartment was within walking distance, but she wasn't stupid enough to walk alone at night, especially after drinking. "Thanks a lot."

Stepping out of Ruby's and into the street-lit parking lot felt oddly surreal. Jed walked close beside her, leading the way toward a shining red car. A Dodge something – she didn't know much about cars, but it looked nice, and it suited Jed.

The seats were leather. She slid onto one, enjoying the glide against the backs of her thighs as Jed held the passenger side door open for her like a perfect, tattoo-covered, sex-exuding gentleman. How the hell was she going to make it through the car ride without embarrassing herself?

"You'll have to give me directions," Jed said as he settled behind the wheel.

She did so, watching the way his hands dwarfed the wheel and the muscles in his forearms shifted as he drove. Light and shadow drifted over his skin from knuckles to elbow as they passed streetlights, taking a turn that had them disappointingly close to her apartment. "It's just up the street here."

Jed slowed the car to a smooth stop by the curb in front of her building.

The leather stuck to the back of her thighs a little, but unfortunately, the hold wasn't strong enough to serve as an excuse not to leave the car. "Thanks for the ride," she said, gathering up her purse and smoothing her skirt. "It was nice not to have to take a cab."

"Anytime." He lowered his hands from the wheel and met her gaze.

Karen's heart did a cartwheel as the atmosphere inside the car changed. Was it just the lemonade coloring her perceptions, or did the air feel suddenly electric? Sitting there with her fingers tangled in her purse strap and her eyes locked with Jed's, she couldn't help but feel like she was balancing on the edge of something.

A sense of the inevitable tingled in her veins, and a voice in the back of her head screamed that she couldn't let the opportunity pass.

Maybe it was just the lemonade, but hell, what were the odds she'd be able to gather enough courage to act any other time? She'd been admiring Jed quietly for months, and quiet was sort of against her nature. Still, she was silent as she leaned forward, lips already burning as she breathed in his scent and the console pressed into her hip…

He moved. In the opposite direction – away from her. Just the tiniest bit, but still. Some part of Karen shriveled up and died of sheer horror as her mind registered the fact that he'd leaned away from her attempted kiss.

She leaned back too, trying to make it seem casual, as if that was even possible. "I, uh, have a brunch date tomorrow. I've gotta get up kind of early. I'd better get to bed…" She squeezed her purse strap so tightly that her knuckles ached. Every fiber of her being urged her to escape the car and the fog of humiliation that had descended upon her, upon the whole evening.

Silent seconds ticked by, and they seemed more like hours as she waited for Jed to respond.

"All right." Two words – they were all he said. And then he leaned forward, across the console and directly into her personal space. Before she could react, his breath was flowing hot against her cheek and his facial hair was scraping the edge of her jaw, causing her spine to tingle and her nipples to harden. There was no mistaking the electricity in the air when his mouth met hers.

At first, his lips were soft. Then they were firm, so hot against hers that she wondered briefly whether he had a fever. But her temperature rose to match his as the kiss continued and his tongue ventured out to skim the edge of her lower lip.

Yielding to the touch was utterly instinctual – something she'd been craving since the first time she'd laid eyes on him. As he slipped his tongue past her teeth, she reached out, pressing a hand against his chest.

His muscle was as rock-hard under her palm as she'd imagined it would be. What tattoos were there, beneath his shirt? She'd never seen, but knew there had to be some. He was tattooed from his hands to his collarbones, from what she could tell. Her speculations blurred as his tongue entwined with hers, melting her attempts at coherent thought.

For a few moments, she simply floated, thinking of nothing besides the heat and pressure of his mouth against hers. And then the kiss was over.

The end seemed abrupt, and the air too cool against her lips, but a slow burn still heated her from the inside.

"I won't keep you," Jed said in a voice so low it rasped against some place deep inside Karen, bringing every nerve she possessed to expectant life.

She breathed, in and out, still tasting him on the tip of her tongue. "Okay." Her voice came out surprisingly steady considering the fact that her head was spinning.

"Have a good time at brunch tomorrow."

"I will. Thanks."

"Happy birthday, Karen." He was still leaning on the console, and his fingers brushed her arm, the touch shockingly sensual for such light contact.

"Happy birthday to you, too."

Her heart practically leapt out of her chest when he exited the car. What was he planning to do ... come inside? It didn't make any sense, given what he'd just said, but the thought had her head spinning even faster and her nerves buzzing.

He opened the passenger side door for her, and her heart rate slowed a little as realization dawned on her. "Thanks." She stepped out, into the night, and looked up at him.

He smiled a smile she would've called conflicted if she'd trusted her judgment, which she didn't – Jed's kiss had been more powerful than any shot. It had left her giddy, happy and bewildered all at once. "Goodnight. I'll see you soon?" She hadn't meant for it to come out as a question, but it did.

"You know you will. Goodnight."

He waited by the curb as she made her way to her second story apartment, and she paused to wave at him before slipping into the privacy of her home, where she was free to sigh, collapse onto the couch and dedicate all her mental efforts to wrapping her mind around the fact that Jed had just kissed her.

Why had he leaned away at first? Why hadn't he tried to take things further? And why, God why, was he so unnaturally good at kissing? No one else had ever made her feel that way with just a kiss...

Nothing made any sense, but that didn't stop her from savoring his heat and taste as both faded slowly from her tongue, leaving a deep craving in their wake.

CHAPTER 3

The sight of Karen's name on the phone screen snared Jed's attention more effectively than an explosion would have. As he accessed his messages, guilt sped through his veins like poison. It was going on six in the evening ... the better part of a day had passed since he'd succumbed to temptation and kissed her the night before. And they hadn't spoken since.

She'd mentioned brunch plans for that morning, and he'd justified the delay in his apology by telling himself he'd probably be interrupting her plans if he tried to get in touch. Truth was, he was fucking procrastinating. Because what could he say that wouldn't drive home the fact that he'd acted like an ass the night before?

I'm printing a ton of stuff right now. Need any more prints for around the shop?

He read her text three times over despite its simplicity, searching for any hidden resentment in her words.

It was impossible, and trying was more than a little pathetic. For a second, he let his finger hover over the call button.

Fuck it. A phone call wouldn't be good enough, either. If she was printing out photos, that meant she was in her photography studio. If he hurried there, he could probably catch her in time to apologize to her face, like she deserved.

No. Thanks though. Listen, I'm sorry about last night.

Even if he was about to see her, he couldn't text her back without at least scratching the surface of the apology he owed her.

?

Her sparse reply burnt itself into his mind, igniting a fresh bout of guilt. If she was trying to say that he owed her more of an explanation, she was right. As he exited the shop with a quick wave to the other artists and receptionist, he tried to stop savoring the memory of having his tongue entwined so thoroughly with Karen's that he could still practically taste her.

His apology would seem a lot more convincing if he completely regretted kissing her, but he didn't – he couldn't.

* * * * *

"Did you hear that?"

"That was a male voice. It was definitely male. Did you hear what it said?"

"I didn't catch any words. It almost sounded like a growl. Let's get back to the lab and check the EVP recording."

Karen leaned back in her chair, adjusting the hydraulic lever beneath the seat. Holy crap, she needed a new desk chair. Why hadn't she bought one yet? That should've been priority number one when she'd started making enough money to do more than just barely pay her bills each month. It was a pain to edit photos – or watch TV online while her printer churned out 5x7s – in the worn out piece of junk-on-wheels.

"Holy crap!" Voices crackled through her cheap computer speakers – another office essential that could use replacing. "Did you hear *that*, man?"

Crappy speakers or no, the EVP recording echoed through Karen's workspace. Ugh, it really did sound like a growl, and they kept replaying it...

Karen glanced toward the window. It wasn't even dark yet, which meant that listening to the static-laced recording alone in her studio shouldn't scare her, not even a little bit.

Still, she jumped and nearly upended her aged desk chair when a knock sounded at the door. Spinning as quickly as her wobbling seat would allow, she turned her back on her computer screen.

Her legs shook as she hurried toward the door. Who could be on the other side? She didn't have any clients scheduled – she'd left the entire day open in order to celebrate her birthday with her grandmother and then get caught up on some odd tasks.

"Karen?" The voice that called from the other side of the door stopped her in her tracks just as her fingertips were about to brush the doorknob.

Memories of the night before rushed back to her, sweet and vivid and a little terrifying when she really thought about them. On the verge of facing Jed for the first time since the kiss, she stood frozen like an idiot with her heart pounding away in her throat. What was about to happen? She let herself wonder for approximately two seconds before she had to stop herself regretting that she hadn't worn sexier underwear.

At least her bra and panties matched – she was reasonably sure of that, although it was kind of hard to remember getting dressed that morning when her thoughts kept zooming back to the memory of Jed's short beard scraping her jaw, his tongue wrapped around hers…

"I'm here." She called out the first thing that came to mind and unlocked the door, opening it to reveal the man she'd barely been able to stop thinking about for the past twenty-four hours.

He looked just like she remembered – sexy as sin – and her already elevated heartbeat sped ahead at the sight. Instead of a button-up with rolled-up sleeves, he wore a black t-shirt. It clung to his muscular torso and revealed the goldmine of well-done ink that covered his arms. "Hey."

"Hey." He stood in the doorway for a moment, silent with his thumbs tucked into his pockets.

She let herself admire him for a few seconds as a cloud of butterflies came to life somewhere between her hips and her heart.

"Can I come in?"

"Sure." She stepped back, unable to resist thinking of his last text. Sorry about last night? What the hell did that mean? Was he sorry he'd kissed her? Sorry he hadn't done more? Wondering had driven her to tune-out in front of her computer screen, courtesy of her favorite ghost hunting show.

He breathed a barely-audible sigh as he strode into the room, looking like he was on the verge of saying something important. Instead, he paused in front of her computer. "You watching this?"

The barest hint of heat crept into her cheeks as she glanced toward the screen, where one of the paranormal investigators was daring a spirit to approach some sort of EMF reader. "I was."

"I had no idea you liked this stuff." Jed's mouth curled in the tiniest of smiles.

"Let me guess – you think it's ridiculous?" Jed wasn't exactly the kind of guy she'd peg as a fan of ghost hunting shows.

He shrugged, his broad shoulders straining his t-shirt in a way so sexy it made her head spin. "I'm just surprised is all. I've never watched more than a few minutes here and there."

"It's a little sensationalistic at times, but the locations they visit are really cool – seeing the historic old places they explore is my favorite thing about the show and—" For once, she stopped herself mid-babble. Forget ghost hunting TV! Who gave a crap about whether the abandoned prison was haunted when there was last night's kiss to discuss, and maybe even relive?

She reached for the mouse and shut off the show. "I won't inflict my reality TV upon you."

"Reality?" Jed arched a dark brow.

Her cheeks warmed a little more. "They *say* it's reality. And I figure it's probably not *all* staged."

"Mmm." Jed was definitely smiling now. "There's no telling, is there?"

"I guess not." Karen turned to her printer and lifted a fresh print from the tray. She wasn't going to argue about the existence of ghosts. Not now, and not with Jed.

The silence that filled the studio was absolute, unrelieved by even a questionable EVP clip now that she'd turned the show off.

"About last night," Jed eventually said, his deep voice banishing the quiet, "I'm sorry. I came here to apologize."

Karen set the print down on her desk, next to the mouse pad, as her pulse fluttered in her fingertips. "Sorry for what?"

* * * * *

She stood there, green eyes wide and hands loose at her sides, her slender fingers brushing the corner of her desk. How could she look so oblivious, like she had no idea what he was talking about?

"For taking advantage of you." He resisted the urge to wince as the words came out. "I shouldn't have kissed you like that – not after you'd been drinking." It had felt right at the time, but that was just evidence of what a fucking creep he was, wasn't it? Offering to give her a ride home after she'd been drinking, and then shoving his tongue down her throat before he let her go...

Karen laughed, and the sound sent slivers of disbelief slicing through him. How could she laugh about it? Had he betrayed her trust so badly that she thought she had to make a show of not caring?

"Jed, you didn't take advantage of me. How could you think that?"

"You'd been drinking," he repeated. "I should've just taken you home, and let that be that."

She crossed her arms, and he couldn't help but notice how the motion pushed up her breasts. Visions of her in her low-cut dress from the night before swarmed his memory and amped-up his guilt. She'd looked amazing... She still did, in the new sweater Mina had given her for her birthday.

"Well, I'm glad you didn't," she said. "I mean yeah, I drank, but not too much. I was barely buzzed, and well – I don't know if I would've been able to work up the courage without a *little* help."

"The courage?"

"To – you know. When I leaned forward and..." Her face was suddenly, totally pink. "I thought we were going to kiss so I sort of leaned toward you. When you pulled away, I was horrified. But then..." She shot him a shy grin. "I realized I'd been right."

"You'd been thinking about us kissing?" The notion sent a pang of sharp-edged desire through him, but he knew he shouldn't savor it ... alcohol had a way of making people think things they shouldn't.

"For *ages*." She crossed her arms a little more tightly, almost as if she were hugging herself. "Ever since I first met you. I just didn't know how... I mean, I was nervous. It was hard for me to tell if you felt the same way."

Looking at her standing that way, with her arms tight around her own body while her eyes searched his, he wanted to pick her up and wrap his own arms around her and hold her so tightly that he'd be able to feel her heart beat, her breasts compressed against his chest... "Are you serious? Karen, I didn't realize..."

Ever since she'd *met* him? Holy shit... That'd been months ago. And yeah, he'd felt an instant attraction too, but the idea that she'd been waiting all that time, wanting something to happen... It was unbelievable. And it made him feel like a dick.

All the excuses he'd found to see her, the way he'd sometimes prolonged their little meetings in the back of the tattoo studio even though she'd answered all his questions and provided better images than he ever could've hoped for... "I feel like I've been leading you on. I'm sorry."

She tightened her self-embrace so much that it was a wonder she could even breathe. "Oh. I see... You *don't* feel the same way." Her face transitioned from pink to red before his eyes, and her expression vacillated from hurt to angry.

Damn it, she looked at him like he'd hit her or something.

"It's not that I'm not attracted to you," he said as his mistake dawned on him. "I am, but it's not like we could be together."

She raised her gaze again, her eyes searching his. "Why not? Are you seeing someone else?"

"No." His voice came out a little too deep, a little too scraping.

"Then what are you talking about?" Her face was still red, but she looked more bewildered than hurt now.

He raised his hands in a useless gesture. "Look at yourself, Karen. You're young, beautiful and successful — on your way to much bigger things than photographing tattoos for my studio, I'm sure. And I'm just myself. I tattoo – that's it; Hot Ink is my life. I don't have anything to offer someone like you."

Karen finally dropped her arms to her sides, where her hands formed loose fists. "Are *you* serious? You don't think you're good enough for me?" She looked at him like she couldn't believe what she was seeing.

"I know I'm not."

"Jed… You're not just saying that because there's some other reason that would hurt my feelings, are you?"

"No."

For a few moments, she just stood there, hands balled and eyes wide. Then she looked around the studio as if searching for something. "Okay, here's the glitz and glamour I'm apparently exuding – see this?" She bent down and picked up something between her finger and thumb.

Or at least, she went through the motions – he couldn't see anything.

"Dog hair," she said. "It's been a freaking week, I've vacuumed twice and I'm still finding it everywhere." She gestured toward her khaki-colored pants. "I've stopped wearing dark colors because the hair shows up so well against them."

"I'm afraid I don't follow."

"Last week I did a shoot for a pet grooming company. Apparently they thought the world's most spastic greyhound would be the perfect model of a well-groomed dog. The shoot was a nightmare – I still have scratch-marks on my arms from that dog, and he peed on the carpet!" She thrust an accusatory finger toward one corner of the room. "Who do you think had to clean it up?"

She shook her head, her mouth set in a firm line. "Anyway, I'm just glad he didn't knock over any of my lights or break anything. In the end, I got a few ad-worthy images, but I worked for them, Jed. I scrubbed *pee-soaked carpet* for them. How's that for bigger and better things?"

"Maybe you should hire an assistant," he suggested. "Someone to help keep a handle on your canine clients and clean up accidents if needed?"

"Don't think I haven't considered it," she said, eyes flashing, "and *don't* try to change the subject. I'm not too good for you, Jed – the idea is ridiculous. So..." Her nerve seemed to falter, and she let her gaze drop. "So don't be sorry about the kiss. I'm not."

A part of him *wasn't* sorry, and that part was rapidly fighting its way to the top. "You'd been drinking and—"

Karen stepped into his personal space as he repeated his earlier argument, struggling to keep a handle on his self-restraint.

A determined look flashed in her eyes as she advanced on him, and he only had a second to wonder what the hell she was doing before reality crashed down on him in the form of her mouth against his.

He hadn't bent, hadn't bowed his head to facilitate what was happening, but she was tall enough that she only had to rock up onto the balls of her feet to reach his mouth. And holy hell, she was a more aggressive kisser than he remembered – there was an edge of fierceness to her kiss, a demand made clear in the way her lips worked against his, surprisingly firm, and then soft...

Her aggressiveness faded as he caved, giving in to the heat and pressure of her mouth, of her body against his. The passion was still there, but they were equals as he wrapped his arms around her, just like he'd imagined. Thoughts of resistance were as far away as the moon as her breasts swelled against his chest, and he could feel the soft flesh conforming to his body. Was he just imagining it, or could he feel her nipples beneath the light sweater she wore?

Imaginary or not, the sensation had him hard as a rock.

"There," she said when she pulled away a full minute later. "I haven't been drinking. Well, okay, I drank at a winery this morning, but that was hours ago."

She was still right up against him, which left the hard rod of his erection stiff against her belly. Her gaze dipped in that direction momentarily, then she met his eyes. "So where does this leave us?" Her lips were swollen from contact with his, and they quirked in a knowing smile – like she knew he couldn't feign resistance.

"I don't know, but I like where we are right now." He rocked his hips just a little, barely able to suppress a moan when his dick slid against her belly. So many layers of clothing between them, and still, the distant friction threatened to kill him with desire. It had been so long, and Karen was like a dream come to life, with her insane curves, swollen lips and pin-up girl red hair...

But she was more than that, too. She was someone he cared about, someone who did not deserve to be dragged down onto a floor that had apparently been violated by the canine star of a recent photo shoot. He pulled away, ignoring the part of him that ached when he lost contact with her body. "If you really want to do this," he said, meeting her eyes, "we should do this right. Can I take you to dinner?"

Her eyes lit up in a way he'd never seen them do before. "Yes."

The part of him that knew he wasn't who she deserved had drowned in her allure, in the reason-crushing hotness of her kiss. And as she slipped one hand into his and grabbed her purse with the other, he couldn't deny that this was exactly what he wanted.

* * * * *

"Can I interest either of you in one of our new after-dinner drinks?" The waiter gestured toward a small fold-out menu propped on the table. "The sweet blackberry wine is—"

"No thanks," Jed said without glancing at the menu. "Just coffee. And maybe some dessert?" He glanced in Karen's direction.

Karen's heart skipped a beat, as it always did when they made eye contact. "Sure." Would it always do that, or would she become used to his company, to his attention? Maybe if she *really* got to know him, her nerves would settle down. Thoughts of exactly how she might go about doing that invaded her mind, vivid and persistent.

As it turned out, neither of them was picky. They settled quickly on the cheesecake.

"I hope you don't mind that I said no to drinks. Whatever happens – I want it to be because you want it, and I don't want to have doubts afterward."

A wave of disbelief crashed down on her. Did he really worry that if she had a glass of wine, she'd have some epic lapse in judgment and end up in some intimate situation she hadn't really desired? If only he could read her mind... "It's fine," she said simply, aware that they were surrounded by dozens of other people. "I'd rather have cheesecake than drinks anyway."

It was no lie – cheesecake was dessert gold, as far as she was concerned.

He smiled a little at that. "Me too."

She grinned back. "See? We really are compatible. I don't know what you were worried about."

The platter the waiter returned with held the single biggest piece of cheesecake Karen had ever seen. Even shared between a couple, the portions were generous. At first she wondered whether they'd finish it, but her doubts evaporated as soon as the first bite touched her tongue.

The cheesecake was rich and silky, so dense that just one bite felt heavy on the end of her fork. And the sweet-tart strawberry sauce that had been spread across the surface... "Oh my God, this cheesecake is amazing."

"It's pretty damn good," Jed agreed a moment later, and they slipped into a comfortable silence.

After Jed paid the check and they left the restaurant, the sense of decadent pleasure inspired by dessert remained. When he pressed a hand gently to the small of her back, the feeling gained an edge of blistering anticipation.

Was all this really happening? After months of fantasizing, tiptoeing around and generally hoping to hell that something more than conversation would unfold between them...

"Where to?" he asked when they slipped into his car.

Karen looked him in the eye and gave him her best attempt at a seductive smile. It felt more awkward than siren-like, and her cheeks heated, but she held his gaze. "I'm open to suggestions. And I'm not ready to go home."

The moment of silence that followed was so heavy she could feel it weighing down on her shoulders, her breasts – her entire body. The pressure was teasing and inspired thoughts of what the weight of Jed's body might feel like against hers.

Was she being brazen? Maybe. But being with Jed – going out with him – didn't feel sudden. She'd been waiting for so long; she'd been admiring him for months. She wanted him, bad – more than she could remember ever wanting anyone else. With any luck, by the time the night was over, he'd realize that, and they could put his absurd doubts behind them.

"We could head back to my place," he said, turning the key in the ignition. "Or we could see a movie."

"I like your first suggestion." Butterflies took flight inside her belly as she spoke, and she sat a little straighter in her seat, practically on the edge of it as she imagined where they were headed.

"I have an apartment above Hot Ink. It's nothing special. You sure you want to head there?" He looked away from the road as he rolled to a stop at the edge of the parking lot.

An electric thrill went through her as his eyes locked with hers. They appeared darker than usual, and they radiated an intensity he'd kept out of his voice.

"Yes." She gripped her purse strap, imagining the feel of Jed's hair between her fingers instead. It was just long enough to run her hands through, to grip – a fact she'd been conscious of ever since the first time they'd met.

CHAPTER 4

As Jed pulled out of the parking lot and onto the street, the car's engine purred, sending slight vibrations through the seats and Karen's body. They struck her breastbone, causing it to tremble beside her heart. The sensation was faint, but steady. She let it course through her system, calming her whirling thoughts.

Jed helped her out of the car when they arrived and together, they made their way to Hot Ink's darkened display windows. The shop had closed an hour ago, and it was strange to walk through the dimmed interior, past empty chairs. There was no telltale buzz of a tattoo in progress, no chatter. Being alone with Jed in a place she was used to seeing full of familiar faces sent a frisson of awareness down her spine.

As they neared a narrow staircase in one of the shop's back corners, she glanced at the door to the dual-purpose office and storage area. A smile tugged at the corners of her mouth as she thought of all the times she'd made excuses to see him there, the little ways she'd found to prolong their conversations.

"Careful – the stairs are a little steep."

They were narrow, too – a fact that created a sense of instant intimacy as they climbed toward the second floor.

Jed unlocked the door at the top of the flight of stairs, and then, Karen was staring square into the home of the man she'd been fantasizing about for months.

She'd spent so much time wondering about him and his life outside of work that everything was interesting, from the little white kitchen table to the red tea kettle sitting on the stove. She would've pegged him as more of a coffee drinker, and discovering something unexpected about him, however trivial, gave her a thrill.

"Nice apartment," she said, and meant it. The building was an older one, and she loved that. His place had so much more character than her modern apartment did. Glancing around, she took in what looked like hand-carved crown molding and the arched doorway that led from the combined kitchen and living area to a hallway.

"It's small, but it's not like I need more room." He closed the door behind them, and Karen savored the small sound that announced that they were alone together in his home.

It happened too fast for her mind to process – one moment they were standing at the edge of the kitchen tile, and then they were in each other's arms, their bodies suddenly and completely entwined. He was hot and already hard against her, causing her head to spin as he pulled her tight against his body, making the embrace they'd shared in her photography studio seem chaste in comparison.

They kissed so deeply and so hard that her lips ached, but that didn't stop her from wanting it to last forever.

It didn't, though. Eventually they pulled apart just enough to breathe, just enough to be able to meet each other's eyes.

There was no question of what would happen next. Karen's entire body was tingling, burning up under the weight of delayed gratification. After all, she'd been imagining this for months. And he was firm against her, his every muscle taut with tension.

Wordlessly, he led her down the short hall and into what seemed to be the only bedroom.

The walls were a dark grey and there was a window above a queen sized bed neatly made with a dark blue comforter. Those things were all she could spare the presence of mind to notice as Jed picked her up like she weighed nothing, swinging her onto the bed and going down with her.

The mattress was softer against her back than he was against her front, and she relished being pressed down into it. When he slipped a hand beneath her sweater, the heat of his fingers against her belly made her nipples go hard, stiffening even more as he slid his hand higher.

She mentally cursed her bra when he caressed her breast, pressing his palm against the swell. Her nipple was aching inside the cup, and having her skin separated from his when he was so close made her want to sigh in frustration. Instead, she snaked a hand around his body, pressed it to the back of his head and buried her fingers in his hair, just like she'd imagined.

The feel of it between her fingers was surprisingly silky, and the solid curve of his skull beneath stood in tantalizing contrast. She curled her fingers, burying them deeper as she exerted pressure, pulling his mouth down to hers.

He came willingly – it wouldn't have worked if he hadn't; he was so much stronger than her. When their lips met, they picked up right where they'd left off, with mouths open and tongues entwined. He flexed his hips against her and his hard cock slid up the inside of her thigh in a promising motion. Even through his jeans and her pants, the feel of it blazed a trail of heat that burned all the way to her core.

When he actually began to remove her clothing, she was reasonably sure she was red from head to toe as a combined result of excitement and blushing. As he stripped her bare, she tried to be helpful, twisting and turning in all the right ways, but was unable to keep her hands off him.

Instead, she pressed them against his shoulders, slid them up and down his chest and even explored the hard ridge straining the front of his jeans. That slowed his progress, but eventually she was naked on the bed.

His eyes glittered, somehow dark and light at once, and she could feel the weight of his gaze on her skin. Still, she didn't waste any time in slipping her hands beneath his shirt, skimming over the firm surface beneath as she leaned in and upward.

She'd been wondering about the ink hidden by his clothing ever since she'd first met him. Slowing for the barest fraction of a second, she savored one last moment of suspense.

He stole the moment away and set her heart racing when he pulled his shirt over his head, tossing it aside.

Karen sat frozen except for her hands, which she moved over his torso, tracing lines and spirals of ink with her fingertips, as if touching would help her take it all in faster.

Lots of ink had been hidden under his shirt, just like she'd imagined. The designs started beneath his collarbones, where two roses had been inked in permanent bloom on his chest, one on the inside of each shoulder. They were a vivid red that stood in contrast to his olive skin and the stark black ink that curled between each flower in a spiraling design, connecting them artfully. And below that...

She sucked in a breath as her gaze was drawn automatically to his abs, the ridges of which she'd previously felt, but never seen. Above the well-defined muscles was a line of looping black ink that cut across his ribs, forming script that said something in another language. Latin? She'd ask later, when she was capable of coherent thought beyond admiring his body.

He put an end to her silent study of his tattoos by unzipping his jeans. The sound of the metal teeth parting caused her core to tighten, and she stared as he stripped, tossing jeans and underwear aside.

He was fully hard, as had been obvious when he'd lain on top of her on the bed, driving her down into the mattress. He looked just as incredible as he'd felt then, and she couldn't resist the urge to reach out and touch.

She let her fingers brush the smooth head of his cock before she wrapped them around his shaft, sighing as she slid her hand to the base and friction heated her hand.

He groaned and flexed his hips, sending his dick a little farther through her grip, so that her fingers rested in the almost-black hair that darkened his groin.

Every muscle inside Karen seemed to clench up, and an ache flared where she craved him, where he wasn't – yet. She slid her hand up and down his shaft, the anticipation building with every stroke, with every hard rush of his breath.

He stopped her with a hand on her forearm, his fingers wrapped easily around her wrist. "I don't—" he growled, cutting himself off with a sharp breath. "Fuck, Karen, I don't have any protection."

Even his grip on her wrist felt good. She let the pleasure of the simple touch flood through her as she considered his words and the scrape of frustration in his voice. "Oh." Disappointment stole into her consciousness, and her heart slammed against her ribs in protest. Stop now? Every fiber of her being screamed in protest. "I forgot all about it, too."

"I'll go out and get some," he said, letting go of her wrist and swinging his legs over the side of the bed. "I'll be back in a little while." His voice dipped a little lower as he reached for his jeans.

Now it was her turn to place a hand on his arm. Summoning the courage, she did exactly that. "I'm on the pill. And uh, I know I don't have any STIs." They'd tested her at her last OBGYN appointment. She hadn't slept with anyone since then – she'd been way too busy fantasizing about Jed to pay much attention to any other men.

He froze with his jeans gripped in both hands, going so still that his hard muscles felt like the stone of a statue beneath her hand. "Same here, but I don't expect you to trust me so blindly. I can go out and buy condoms."

She eyed his jeans, then the rigid form of his cock rising from his lap. It was hard to imagine him getting into his pants without being in pain, and then there was the agony of delayed gratification…

How could she not trust the man who'd tried to pay her more for her photography when she owed him so much, who'd been hesitant to go out with her in the first place because of the ludicrous idea that he wasn't good enough for her? Hell, he'd apologized for taking advantage of her because of a single kiss. He wouldn't lie to her, especially not about something so serious. "I trust you, Jed."

"Still." He didn't continue dressing, but he didn't drop his jeans, either.

Realization dawned on her, sending heat creeping into her cheeks. "If you don't feel safe, we don't have to go without protection. Maybe I could get tested again some other time, and share the results with you."

"It's not that. I believe you."

"Then what is it?"

A moment of silence ticked by before his jeans finally fell to the floor with a muffled sound. "It's nothing."

For someone who'd been completely still for a full minute, he moved with amazing speed. He had his arms around her in an instant, and next thing she knew, he was pressing her down into the mattress again, only this time there was nothing between them.

Her pussy clenched as the weight of his embrace registered with her mind and body, blowing a few circuits somewhere in the sensory cortex of her brain. Her nipples were rock hard against his chest, and she could feel him breathe, feel his heart beat. His erection was between her thighs, the head brushing her already-slick skin, and it was hard to believe they were so close.

Though they were on the verge of finally being really, fully together, it didn't happen as quickly as it could have. Instead of entering her, he drew back a little, lowering his head to her chest and mouthing the swell of one breast.

She trembled beneath him, then gasped when he finally closed his lips around the tip, sucking it deep into his mouth.

The pressure of his jaw against her flesh and the scrape of his facial hair against her skin made her arch against the bed, suddenly breathless.

He placed his hands on her breasts, squeezing and rubbing her other nipple with his fingertips, causing it to go just as hard as the one that was caught between his tongue and teeth. Ripples of pleasure raced up and down her spine, through her entire body, and she could barely breathe. When she did, she had to draw air in deep drafts, and still, it wasn't enough.

When he stopped, she let her muscles go slack, lying flat against the mattress as she told herself that she really wasn't melting, it just felt that way. In the wake of what he'd just done, her breasts felt heavy and her nipples hyper-sensitive – so much so that even the motion of him pulling his hands from them made her gasp.

"You're so beautiful," he said, still on top of her but with his hands at her sides, resting on the comforter. "Jesus, I can hardly stand it."

His words burrowed deep inside her mind, into a place where they'd stay forever – she'd never be able to forget him saying that. It was a thrill, but it also sent a pulse of shyness through her that nothing else had. The yin and yang of the effects left her feeling slightly giddy, and she focused on the feeling of his hard thighs between hers.

"Don't look away." He slipped a hand beneath her chin and exerted gentle pressure.

She let him guide her gaze back to his, and after a couple moments of stillness, he began to lower himself.

He didn't break eye contact, just slid lower, until it was his shoulders against the insides of her thighs, not his legs. It was obvious what he was about to do, and she couldn't find it in herself to say a word, encouraging or otherwise. Instead, she focused all her mental energy on steeling herself for it, on trying to figure out how she'd make it through without simply shattering as a result of the pleasure that was already rising up inside her.

He pressed his mouth to her pussy with the same abandon he'd shown her breasts. The heat and moisture of his tongue and lips against her folds was like something out of a dream, only better – better even than the most delicious daydreams she'd managed to come up with over the past few months, all starring Jed. As he dipped his tongue into her entrance, she arched against the bed again, thrusting her hips against his mouth.

In response, he dragged his tongue upward, over her swollen clit.

If she'd had her eyes open, she wouldn't have been surprised if she'd seen stars. The contact was that shocking. At the same time, it was exactly what she'd expected – electricity and bliss all rolled up in one, with a sharp edge of desire that demanded, more, more, more…

When he gave her thigh a squeeze, she realized she'd whispered the request out loud.

The hair on his jaw was just coarse enough to make her skin pebble when it scraped against her pussy, teasing her where his tongue wasn't. When he focused his attention on her clit, realization hit her hard – she was about to come. In Jed's bed, with Jed's mouth on her body and Jed's shoulders between her thighs…

She glanced down at the span of his inked shoulders splitting her legs and a shudder of delight tore through her. He was so sexy it almost hurt to look at him, and this was only a partial view. Tension was wound tight in her core, and as her head spun and her gaze roved over the ink sprawled across his skin, it began to unravel.

She lost control at the exact moment he dragged his tongue upward over her clit, his jaw pressing into her folds below. He didn't hold back, and neither did she – she couldn't have, even if she'd wanted to – as her climax crashed down on her.

The muscles in her core tightened, loosened a little and tightened again, pulsing as she gasped, losing every last bit of air in her lungs. She couldn't help writhing a little, but Jed held her steady with a hand on each thigh, working his tongue against her clit like getting her off was the only thing in the world he gave a damn about.

After a breathless peak, the ecstasy ebbed slowly, a less intense pleasure lingering in its place.

When he rose from between her thighs, he licked one shining-wet lip with the tip of his tongue as he met her eyes.

"That was amazing," she barely managed to breathe.

A distinct light passed through his eyes, gone in a flash, and he leaned in, like he was going to settle between her thighs and finally take her in earnest.

She wanted that – she wanted it so badly she ached at the thought – but she wanted other things, too. Mainly, to do for Jed what he'd just done for her, or at least come as close as she could. He might not see them as equals yet, but she knew better and after the pleasure he'd just given her, it would be no easy task to outshine his generosity – or his skill – in bed.

Willing all of her energy into her jelly-like limbs, she pulled her legs under herself and scrambled into a kneeling position, stopping with her nose almost bumping his chest.

"What are you doing?" He looked down, head bowed as he knelt in front of her.

"Something I've been daydreaming about for six months," she said, and lowered her head into his lap before the heat that rushed into her cheeks could manifest itself in a visible blush.

He drew in a sharp breath when she pressed her lips to the head of his cock, and his hands went immediately to her back.

A little sweet and a little salty, his skin was hot and velvet-smooth against the tip of her tongue as she prepared to take him in. First, she traced the ridge at the edge of the head of his dick, memorizing the broad curve of it before closing her lips around his shaft.

She hadn't expected the pressure and bite of his hands in her hair, his fingers wrapped and tangled against her skull. The element of surprise made it that much hotter, and her pussy tightened as she squeezed her eyes shut, focusing on the feel and sound of him, on everything they were doing.

He kept his hands wrapped in her hair, but he didn't force her, didn't even guide her, just anchored her to him in a way that let her feel his tension, his anticipation.

When she took him deeper of her own volition, he groaned, and the sound vibrated through all of her, making her nerves buzz. As she continued, she braced one hand against his hip. His muscles were like steel beneath her hand, and feeling that sent little shivers up and down her spine as she took him as far as she could.

He tightened his fists in her hair, but he'd gripped large enough handfuls that it didn't really hurt. Heat raced through her as she slid up and down his shaft, running her tongue along the underside, caressing him and enduring every wrenching contraction that rippled through her core as she imagined what it would be like to have him there.

For the first time, he utilized his hold on her hair, exerting gentle pressure to still her as he pulled back his hips, easing out of her mouth.

He didn't say anything, but she read the signs of what would come next in his touch – the way he withdrew his hands from her hair but placed them just as purposefully against her shoulders – and in the way he looked at her.

His gaze was so intense it felt like he was looking deep into her, divining secrets that made her heart beat faster just to think about. Did he know how badly she wanted him, how she'd made so many excuses to see him over the past six months, how thoughts and fantasies of him had lingered in her consciousness for days after each time she'd left Hot Ink?

Maybe he did, and maybe he'd felt the same way about her, because as he eased her down onto the bed and laid his body flush against hers, he sighed like he'd just gotten something he'd waited an eternity for.

She made a similar sound, wrapping her arms around him and pressing her hands to his back as he settled between her thighs.

He fit perfectly there, and she fought a tremor of anticipation as the head of his dick nudged the still-damp lips of her pussy. For half a second, they were still that way, with his hardness hot at the threshold of her ready body. And then he flexed his hips, pushing past her slick skin and into her aching core.

She'd dreamed of feeling him inside her, and the tight bands of muscle that embraced him now had been contracting in anticipation ever since he'd first laid hands on her. But the reality of feeling her body yielding to the broad shaft of his cock shattered her fantasizes and stole her breath. He slid deeper and deeper, going all the way on the first stroke. The unrelenting pressure of the head of his dick so far inside her ached in a way that permeated her entire body, not just the core of her, where he was.

For a few moments, she was still as pleasure made her dizzy. Breathing in a deep lungful of his scent, she dared to rock her hips, urging him to continue.

He pulled back slowly, retreating some but remaining firmly inside her, and rocked deep again as he bowed his head, pressing his mouth against hers.

She arched against the mattress as the softness of his lips and scrape of his short facial hair teased her into borderline-madness. When she let him in, he let his tongue delve into the far depths of her mouth.

Letting her fingers curl, she dug her nails into his back and clung to him as coherent thought faded away and some primal, happy part of her took over. Faint bolts of warning arced through her belly and she welcomed them, focusing on the promise of ecstasy they carried.

Each time Jed rocked into her, he hit a place deep inside her, and his body rubbed against her ultra-sensitive clit. Between the physical stimulation and the mental high created by his embrace, his scent and the sound of the bed groaning beneath them, she was amazingly, breathlessly sure that she'd reach climax.

They were still kissing when the first tell-tale ripple rolled through her, causing her pussy to seize up around his dick. She gasped and he groaned at the same time, causing their mouths to slip apart. She hardly had time to miss the pressure of his mouth against hers; her second orgasm pulled her in like a riptide, and it was all she could do to ride out the wave, unable to spare a thought for anything else.

He thrust harder into her, sighing her name as the contractions intensified.

Coming with his mouth against her clit had been amazing; climaxing with him inside her was a million times better. The rock-hard presence of his cock gave her pussy something to tighten around, something to embrace as her body reciprocated pressure for pressure and pleasure for pleasure. As she continued to gasp, his breath rushed against her face and rippled through her hair, hot and ragged.

After a few breathless moments at her peak, she crashed back down into the reality of still being in his arms and still experiencing pleasure, though she was suddenly exhausted. Her breathing slowed a little and hitched as he continued to rock into her with steady but increasingly fast strokes. Everything inside her seemed to melt as he breathed her name again, punctuating it with a hard thrust that sent echoes of her recent orgasm through her body, making her arch beneath him.

The aftershocks of her climax continued as he came, driving himself into her with unmistakable purpose. His pleasure was her pleasure, too; feeling him lose himself wasn't the same sort of bliss as a climax of her own, but it rivaled that sort of satisfaction.

They stayed together for a few moments after he stilled, locked in the position in which he'd stolen her breath so many times that she'd lost count. When he withdrew, he settled beside her and cupped her face in one hand, gently turning her head until their gazes locked.

His eyes were intense, maybe even curious, almost as if he was searching for something in hers. Maybe he found whatever he'd been looking for, or maybe not – he didn't say, just wrapped an arm around her and pulled her close.

Quiet moments passed by, warmed by the heat of their bare bodies. Karen let herself sink into the feeling of intense satisfaction that lingered inside her, her gaze sweeping idly over Jed's perfect body. Even after what they'd just done, the sight of him naked still made her spine tingle. She traced swirling lines of ink with her gaze, and one pattern – one word – in particular captured her attention.

Alice, the scrolling, loopy script that had been inked up his right side read. It was a simple tattoo, pretty and perplexing. Who was Alice? She wondered for a few brief moments before dismissing the thought.

There was a story behind every tattoo – Jed had told her that once – and the story behind a woman's name obviously wasn't one she was going to request as she lay naked in his arms. Instead, she brushed a fingertip lightly over the first word of the phrase that curved around his left ribcage, from front to back. "This is Latin, right?"

He nodded.

"What does it say?"

He swept a stray lock of hair out of her eyes, letting his fingers linger behind her ear. "*Sic transit gloria mundi.* Thus passes the glory of the world."

CHAPTER 5

The whisper of Karen's bare feet against the hallway carpet might as well have been gunfire. It captured Jed's attention that effectively, reminding him that he wasn't alone. He was so used to having the apartment to himself that any foreign sound rushed through the rooms and bounced off the walls, echoing inside his head.

"Morning," he said, pulling an electric skillet out of the cupboard beside the fridge. He'd been up for maybe five minutes – long enough to pull on a pair of jeans and brush his teeth. She'd been sound asleep when he'd left her curled in his bed, tangled in the sheets.

"Morning." She swept through the living area and into the kitchen, her thighs bare beneath the hem of one of his t-shirts.

"Thought I'd make breakfast." He glanced at her over his shoulder as he reached blindly into a cupboard and pulled out a box of baking mix. He didn't need sight to find it – no one but him touched anything in the kitchen;

he always knew where everything was. "You like pancakes?"

"Love them." She approached the table with a little twirl, faltering slightly on the slick tile and steadying herself with a hand on the back of one chair. "Need any help cooking?" she asked, half laughing.

"Morning person, are we?" he asked, taking in the bright shine of her green eyes and the straightness of her spine as she stood poised beside the table, her hair cascading over her shoulders in rumpled auburn waves. He teased, but she looked more alive than anyone else he'd ever seen less than a minute out of bed.

She awoke something in him, too – namely, his cock, which stiffened a little at the sight of his t-shirt clinging to her breasts and her mile-long legs bared beneath.

"I like mornings." She let her hand slip from the chair and approached the counter, where he stood. "It's the most peaceful part of the day, if you ask me. Not tired peaceful, though – exciting peaceful. When I get up, a part of me sort of feels like anything could happen."

"Wish I could say the same." Exciting wasn't exactly how he'd describe his feelings while brushing his teeth, shuffling around the normally quiet kitchen and finding something to eat while blinking the grit and heaviness of sleep out of his eyes.

"Want me to put some water on for tea?"

Her words went through him cold and fast, like a mouthful of ice water. Gripping the box of baking mix in one hand and a bowl in the other, he turned to see her holding the red teapot aloft, her slender fingers curled around the handle as she eyed him and then the nearby faucet.

"Actually, I drink coffee." He set the bowl down on the counter, and the sound seemed absurdly loud.

"Oh." She lowered the teapot back onto the rear left stove burner, the one he never used.

"I'll put some coffee on. Do you drink it?"

"Yeah. I just saw the teapot and figured you didn't."

"It was my wife's." He poured too much baking mix into the bowl, then turned away to fetch eggs anyway, leaning into the fridge as the chill crept over his skin. He knew damn well that Karen probably didn't know about Alice, and that sticking his head in the refrigerator was an idiotic thing to do. Still, he didn't want to watch her face transform when he dropped the bomb on her.

"I didn't know you were ever married." Already, her voice was a little softer than before.

"For ten years. Lost Alice five years ago."

"Oh, Jed." The whisper-soft noise of her feet against tile rang in his ears again, strangely loud. "I'm so sorry. I had no idea."

She was so close now that he felt the heat radiating from her body. Straightening, he stood and closed the fridge, a carton of eggs cradled in one arm. "It was cancer."

"No one ever mentioned it. I—"

"It's all right." A pang of guilt struck him deep in his chest as he met her eyes. They were so wide, still shining, but not with her early-bird cheerfulness. "I just didn't want to keep it a secret. Everyone else knows." Most or all of Hot Ink's staff, anyway. Maybe not Mina, who'd only been working in the shop for a few months, but the rest... James and Tyler had known Alice, and the others had been there long enough to hear the stories.

"I feel terrible for bringing it up."

"Don't. If I couldn't bear thinking about her, I'd have put the teapot away. You're fine."

"Okay." She didn't say anything else about it, but she stayed close by his side and helped him make the pancakes even though it was so easy that two people complicated the process more than simplified. He didn't mind the closeness, the rubbing of elbows and the soft whip of her t-shirt hem against his thigh. But he minded the way her sunniness had disappeared, replaced by a more somber version of the Karen who'd twirled up to the table just minutes ago.

As they ate the pancakes and sipped coffee together, she blushed a little when she told him how much she'd enjoyed the night before. Her words and the way she looked up at him from beneath her lashes were enough to make him fully hard beneath the table. Still, he didn't dare take her in his arms and loose himself in loving her again, because the sunlight that filtered through the nearest window illuminated the way she checked her smiles, the way she glanced at him every now and then as if searching his face for something that worried her.

He should never have brought her back to his apartment. Five years had passed since Alice's death, but the place was still a museum of his grief; the kitchen alone held so many of her things, from the teapot to the little drawer full of decorative towels to the old tins of loose leaf tea that lurked in the back of a cupboard. He didn't use any of them, but he didn't get rid of them, either – how could he?

Karen was brighter and warmer than the sunlight that backlit her, lending her hair a fiery sheen. It had been wrong of him to bring her to a place where she felt the need to suppress herself and whatever happiness she possessed, and it was wrong of him to keep her there. When she said that she had a Sunday afternoon portrait session she needed to prepare for, he did his best to ignore the stabbing feeling of longing the idea of her departure filled him with.

As he waited at the table while she dressed in the bedroom, being alone in the kitchen didn't feel as natural as it usually did.

When she paused at the door and pressed her mouth gently against his, he fell back into the trap of passion, completely and selfishly. For a few moments, he kissed her deeply, until he thought his lips might bruise. His cock was hard, aching like the rest of him, and her body was so soft and hot against him that he had to remind himself why he couldn't just keep her there, pressed against the doorframe, forever. Mentally cataloguing all of Alice's kitchen items, he pictured Karen as she'd looked when she'd apologized for offering to make tea.

"Are you closing the shop tonight?" she asked when he finally ended the kiss and pulled back.

"Yeah. I'm opening too, in about two hours. That leaves plenty of time for me to give you a ride home."

"Thanks."

His feelings of guilt hadn't faded by the time he pulled up in front of her apartment building. There, he clutched the wheel as he remembered his first impulsive, selfish mistake – kissing her instead of letting her walk inside untouched. He made the same mistake again, stroking his tongue along the seam of her mouth and inside, where it entwined with hers, before she opened the passenger side door.

"You mind if I give you a call tonight, after I close up?" he asked, knowing he couldn't not say anything.

She smiled, and her genuine expression wrenched something deep inside him painfully. "I'll talk to you then."

He watched her climb the stairs and disappear into her apartment. Alone again, he pulled away from the curb and tried to figure out what he'd say to her that night, how he could possibly convey the truth — which was that he had nothing to offer her — in a way that she'd believe.

* * * * *

Karen sank into her desk chair and breathed a sigh of contentment. It was so nice to shoot reasonable, poseable human beings. Much better than hyperactive greyhounds. Her client — a highschool girl — and her mother had just left the studio, and there wasn't a trace of pee or silver hair anywhere. Popping the SD card out of her camera, Karen prepared to spend an hour or two going through the images from the senior portrait session, choosing the best and beginning editing work.

She'd barely tagged three especially good images when her phone vibrated against the surface of the desk.

Her heart gave a little leap as she reached for it, her mind awash with memories of Jed's touch, Jed's heat, Jed's voice... Hot Ink wasn't due to close for a couple hours, but she couldn't help but wonder whether he might be calling her early during a break. Who cared that she'd seen him just that morning? Remembering their time together was like a natural high, and she couldn't wait to see him again, to do it all over again.

It wasn't Jed. A potent little bolt of disappointment shot through her as she eyed the unfamiliar number. 212 – what area code was that? Not a Pittsburgh one.

"Hello?" She answered the call, still half-lost in thoughts of Jed.

"May I speak with Karen Landry?"

"That's me." She drummed her fingertips against her desktop, eyeing two very similar shots. The girl's smile was a little wider in one, but they both flattered her.

"This is Emma Day-Rogers. I'm calling on behalf of Marc St. Pierre Bridal."

Karen's heart leapt into her throat and she immediately stopped drumming her fingers on the desk, gripping the edge instead as her pulse pounded in her ears. "Yes?"

"We're pleased to inform you that your entry in our Elegant Bride Photography Contest has passed the final round of judging and has been chosen as the winner."

Somehow, Karen resisted the urges to scream into the phone and / or pass out on the spot. Gripping the phone hard, she managed some kind of response and spent the next fifteen minutes jotting down all the details Emma gave her, asking questions here and there and confirming that yes, she was able to travel during the set dates. By the time the conversation was over, she felt like she was floating on a cloud, high above the skyline.

Mina was at work, so Karen dialed Hot Ink's number, spinning in her desk chair as she waited for her to pick up.

The sound of her best-friend's voice sent her excitement spiking to new levels. "Mina! Guess what?"

"What?" She lowered her voice to a half-whisper. "Did you finally get together with Jed this weekend?"

Karen took a deep breath as memories of doing exactly that hit her again. "Yes, but that's not what I'm calling about."

"Okay, what's so exciting that you're skipping telling me about your date with Jed?"

"You know those photos you let me take of you in your wedding gown for that contest?"

"Yeah."

"I won! I won the contest, Mina. I get to go to New York in a couple weeks to shoot a spread for Marc St. Pierre's winter bridal catalogue!" It was the first time she'd said it out loud, and she found herself half-shouting despite her best efforts to contain her enthusiasm.

"Karen, that's amazing! Congratulations."

Karen forced herself to exhale slowly. "Thanks again for posing for those photos. This is going to be amazing for my portfolio. I mean, Marc St. Pierre! What a tear sheet!"

"I bet this will open all kinds of doors for you, Karen. I can't wait to see the photos."

"I can't wait to take them. I'm so excited I don't know what to do with myself. I can't edit images right now – I can't even sit still."

"I'm working tonight because I was just getting home from the fieldtrip this morning, but I'll be off work in a couple hours when the shop closes. Let's meet for a drink to celebrate. It'll be just the two of us – Eric went home an hour ago, so he'll be there for Jess if she needs anything."

"That sounds great. Ruby's?"

"Of course."

"Call me when you're on your way."

"All right."

Karen ended the call and prepared to make another, but stopped before doing so. Why should she sit in her studio talking on the phone when she could head over to her grandmother's place? If there had ever been news worthy of an in-person visit, this was it. And if she knew her grandmother, they'd open one of the bottles of wine she'd brought home from the winery the day before and have a glass of something sweet to celebrate.

She exited her studio, locking up and racing down to her car in the lot below with record speed. Once she was behind the wheel, she made straight for her grandmother's condo.

There, as she climbed the building's stairs, she could practically taste wine on the tip of her tongue. Maybe the pink moscato they'd tried yesterday – they'd both liked that, and her grandmother had purchased a couple bottles.

The condo was on the second level. When Karen neared the unit, she was greeted by a familiar figure. "Hi, Sylvia."

The woman stood in the open doorway of her own unit, bracing herself with a hand against the doorframe. As Karen approached the open door, preparing to pass, she came close enough to see that Sylvia's grip on the wooden frame was tight and white-knuckled. "Is everything okay?"

There was an uncharacteristic tightness about the middle-aged woman's features, too – a few lines in places that were normally smooth. Apprehension crept into Karen's gut and stopped her in her tracks, where she was uncomfortably aware that she was the sole recipient of Sylvia's undivided attention.

Karen knew Sylvia well enough to realize that this wasn't her normal behavior – Sylvia had lived in the unit neighboring her grandmother's for a couple years. She'd even joined Karen and Helen for pie and coffee a couple times.

"I wanted to call you," Sylvia said, her lips bright pink against a pale face. "I didn't know your number."

"What's wrong?" Karen gripped her purse handle like a lifeline and resisted the urge to rush to her grandmother's door and knock until it was opened to her. "Why would you need to call me?"

"Your grandmother had an… A heart attack, I think. I'm no doctor, but the walls are thin enough that I heard her cry out for help. I hurried over and she was complaining of chest pain. I called 911 right away."

Oh my God. The words echoed through Karen's mind, but didn't come out. Pressing her lips together, she summoned her voice. "How long ago was this?"

"The ambulance left about ten minutes ago."

Karen's head spun as a distinct feeling of sickness settled over her. Should she be grateful? Panicked? She was both, and terrified on top of it. "What hospital?"

"Allegheny General."

As Karen turned on her heel, Sylvia reached for her. "I can drive you. Do you need a ride?"

"That's all right. I can drive myself." She didn't – couldn't – trust anyone else to drive fast enough. Jogging, she was nearly to the staircase before her mind caught up with her instincts. "Thank you," she called over her shoulder, "thank you so much for helping her."

She charged down the steps, not waiting for Sylvia's answer, and rushed across the parking lot, only minutes behind the ambulance that had taken one of the most important people in her life.

* * * * *

A shadow slipped over Jed's empty tattoo chair, and he knew it wasn't a client – none were scheduled, and he'd have heard a walk-in. "Everything okay?" He looked up and caught Mina's reflection in the mirror that lined the back wall of his half-booth.

One second of eye contact in the mirror and it was obvious everything wasn't.

"Sorry Jed, but would it be all right if I left early? Karen's grandmother had a heart attack and is in the hospital in critical condition. Karen's there alone – her parents live in Scranton."

Scranton was on the other side of the state – Jed didn't need to do the math to know that unless someone went, Karen would spend an agonizing night alone in the hospital. "Yeah, of course you can go. I'll take care of any walk-ins."

The day was almost done anyway – Hot Ink was scheduled to close in just over an hour.

Mina thanked him and Jed watched her leave, still in his half-booth as he wracked his mind for some reason – any reason – to go with her.

But Mina had a car; she didn't need a ride. And Karen didn't need him, anyway – not when she'd have her best friend. Mina knew Karen much better than he did.

That didn't stop him from aching to be there for Karen. He knew exactly what it was like to spend the night in a hospital, not truly alone, but alone in every way that counted, keeping watch over someone as you tried to convince yourself that they even knew you were there. It made his gut clench and his head ache to imagine Karen going through that.

"Hey, Tyler." He turned to the only other person left in the shop. "Let's close up early. Neither of us have got anything else scheduled." There wasn't really enough time left to deal with any walk-ins, and he'd be shit for tattooing for the rest of the night, anyway.

Tyler seemed happy enough to check out ahead of time, and Jed closed the shop without fanfare, locking the doors, flipping the sign to 'closed' and making a pathetic attempt at paperwork before he shut off the lights and headed upstairs.

The usual, almost-comfortable solitude of his apartment had vanished. In its wake was a conscious emptiness, a feeling that reminded him the place was just a shell of the less lonely times he'd shared with others inside its walls. Alice, Karen – he thought of them both as he sank onto the couch.

It seemed stupid now – selfish, somehow – that less than an hour ago, his biggest concern had been how he could get Karen to see what a mistake they'd made by sleeping together, by beginning a romance that was destined to disappoint her. Those things were true, but he still cared about her and knew he'd lie awake that night, thinking of her suffering at a hospital bedside.

The fact that he'd promised to call her hadn't slipped his mind, either, but she had enough on her plate without him interrupting. Pulling his phone from his pocket, he composed a text instead. She could read it whenever she got a chance.

Mina told me what happened. Sorry. Let me know if there's anything I can do – call anytime.

He hit send and tried to will away the vague feeling of disgust that settled over him. 'Let me know if there's anything I can do' - people had said that to him over and over when he'd been dealing with Alice's illness, and then afterward, when he'd been left alone. There was nothing anyone could've done – no amount of well-wishing could save a life, or reverse the crippling devastation of a loss.

He knew that, and still, he ached to do *something* for Karen. He knew better than most how useless those feelings were, but he couldn't stop them, just like he couldn't stop wanting Karen even though he knew he shouldn't.

* * * * *

A reflection in one of the hospital's windows showed Karen that she was red-eyed. Pretty bad if she could tell that from a darkened likeness of herself, but her appearance was the last thing that mattered right now. "You can go home, Mina. Really. Get some sleep."

"What are you going to do?"

"The same thing, I guess." At least, she'd try. She was exhausted, but she didn't expect sleep to come easily when she got back to her apartment.

"Now that my parents are here…" She trailed off as she and Mina stepped outside, into the early morning chill that defied the heat that would come later in the day. The dawn was beautiful breaking over the city, but she shielded her eyes against the widening sliver of orange on the horizon.

"I hate the thought of you being all alone in your apartment. I'd be happy to stay with you, or you can come back to my place, if you'd prefer."

"It's really okay." They crossed the parking lot, pausing for a car that crept by at a low speed. "I know my dad is officially in charge of arrangements, but I want to help. So I'm going to try to get some rest while I can." Her mind felt trapped in a fog; she wasn't sure if she craved clear-headedness or not, but she hadn't slept all night, and knew she wouldn't be much help shuffling around like a zombie.

"Okay, but only if you're sure."

Karen downed the last sip of the cold coffee she'd been carrying around in a Styrofoam cup for the past hour. "I'm sure. Thanks for staying the night with me."

"No problem. Do you want me to drive?"

"That's all right." They climbed into Karen's car and began a quiet drive away from the hospital.

* * * * *

"How's Karen's grandmother? How's Karen?" Jed didn't bother trying to seem casual when Mina walked through Hot Ink's front door shortly before noon on Monday.

"Not good," Mina said, looking up with a frown. The whites of her eyes were streaked with red, and there were circles beneath them. "Her grandmother died within a few hours of arriving at the hospital. I stayed there with her until dawn – her parents are taking care of things now."

Her words hit him like a blow to the gut, and he couldn't help but remember Karen smiling just days before as she'd texted her grandmother, accepting a dinner invitation. Had they been close?

"Where's Karen now?"

"She said she was heading back to her apartment."

"Alone?"

Mina nodded. "I offered to go with her, but she said she'd be okay." A little dent appeared in her lower lip as she bit it from the inside. "I don't know, though. Years ago, when the accident happened and Jess was in the hospital, after they released me as a patient ... I didn't spend much time at home, but when I went to the apartment to shower, change clothes or whatever – I felt so alone."

Jed nodded.

"Of course, Jess made it out of the hospital, eventually. I guess I don't really know what Karen's going through."

"You don't have to work today, Mina. Go home and get some sleep. I'll call Zoe and ask her to come in. If she can't, well survive for a day without a receptionist."

Mina shook her head. "If Karen doesn't need me around, I might as well be here. I got a couple hours of sleep after coming home from the hospital – if I go to bed now, it'll mess with my sleep cycle."

He tried to convince her to take the day off, but she was adamant.

The hours dragged by. It took all Jed's willpower to focus on the task at hand when one of his regulars came in for a scheduled appointment. After an hour and a half of work, he was left with no client. His mind wandered, his worries for Karen merging with memories of the first few days after Alice's death.

"Hey guys," Mina said, standing in the aisle between the half-booths during a mid-afternoon lull. "Karen just texted me. She said the service for her grandmother is scheduled for Thursday. I think it would mean a lot to her if we all went. She and her grandmother were really close."

"I'll close the shop during the service hours that day. Mina, can you post an update on our site and cancel any appointments?"

Mina nodded. "Sure. And thanks." She walked slowly back to the front desk and began clicking away on the laptop that sat to the side of the register.

"Hell, I'm gonna go pick up some coffee." Jed rose from the stool inside his half-booth. "What does everyone want?"

He walked out with Mina, James and Abby's orders written down on a scrap of paper. It only took a minute to make it to the coffee place across the street. It seemed like everyone was there for an afternoon pick-me-up. He stood in line, images of Karen flashing through his mind.

What was she doing now? She had to be awake – she'd just texted Mina. The barista waved him forward, and on an impulse, he ordered an extra of Mina's preferred drink.

He'd just have to hope that she and Karen had similar tastes. Whatever Karen was doing, she had to be tired. So after dropping off most of the coffees at Hot Ink, he left again.

Maybe Karen wasn't even home. He'd find out soon enough. As he settled behind the wheel of his Charger, all he was certain of was that he had to do something, however small, to try to ease Karen's pain. Especially since he knew exactly how she felt. If she didn't want his company, she could at least have the coffee.

CHAPTER 6

She was home. In fact, she answered the door the first time he knocked. Her eyes were red and circled like Mina's, but she still looked beautiful.

"Jed. I had no idea you were planning to stop by." She stood in the doorway, eyes widening a little.

"Hope you don't mind. I thought you'd be tired after last night – brought you some coffee."

"Wow, thanks." She surprised him by smiling as she accepted the cardboard cup.

"Do you like vanilla?"

"Who doesn't?" She took a sip of the latte.

Jed stood there for several quiet moments, a sense of awkwardness creeping up on him. "Is there anything else I can do?"

She frowned a little and shook her head. "I don't even know what I'm doing. Just waiting for something to do, I guess. Tomorrow I'm going to pick out flower arrangements for the funeral service. Until then..." She shrugged, looking helpless. "I don't think it's really hit me yet."

He nodded. The human mind didn't just wrap itself around the absence of someone it cared about the instant a life was lost. It didn't work like that – grief was like an onion, many-layered and potent, proving you wrong when you thought there were no more tears left.

"Everyone from Hot Ink will be at the service," he said. "I don't know if Mina's told you yet, but I'm closing the shop so everyone can attend."

She flashed him another little smile. "Thanks."

Several silent moments ticked by, and he cursed himself inside his head. Why wasn't he better at this? He'd been through it himself, for fuck's sake, and hadn't forgotten how it felt.

"Do you want to come in?" she asked, stepping aside.

"Only if you'd like me to."

"I would. The quiet's been driving me crazy these past few hours. With my parents handling things for the day, I don't know what to do. I can't edit photos, can't work on my website – every time I try to do something useful, I can't concentrate." She pressed the cup to her lips again, meeting his gaze over the rim.

"It can be hard." He pulled the door shut behind himself as he entered her apartment for the first time. There were black and white art prints on the walls – lots of them. Landscapes, skylines and portraits, many of which were familiar.

"I didn't know you displayed any of these in your home." He nodded toward a dramatically-lit shot of a man's back, the focus of which was a sea of ink, complete with a ship sailing at full mast.

"Yeah. Some of my favorites, anyway."

He scanned the portraits, satisfaction settling a little deeper into his bones each time he spotted a photo of one of his clients. Looked like most of her favorites were his work. "You have good taste."

She smiled faintly. "Do you want to watch a movie or something? I was thinking of putting one in."

"Sure." He'd do whatever she wanted. He held no delusions about his role in her life at the moment – he was there just to be there for her, to do whatever would help put her at ease.

"I was thinking a comedy. Nothing too serious. What kind of movies do you like?"

"I'll watch just about anything."

The couch was a loveseat. It was pretty standard for a single person's small apartment. It also put him noticeably close to Karen when he sat down. He settled on one end, with an arm on the rest, but they were still close enough that he could feel the heat radiating from her body.

He tried not to think about it and willed himself not to notice the scent of her freshly-washed skin. It was strong, though – she must have showered recently. Damn it, it was hard not to picture that. In his mind's eye, he could see hot water rushing over the curves he'd gotten to know less than 48 hours ago.

"Hope you haven't seen this one already," she said, scooting into the center of the couch and leaning against him as the movie started.

"Nope," he said, trying not to tense as her breast pressed against his bicep, soft and warm. Damn it, how was he supposed to watch the movie like a normal person with her draped over his side?

It was a selfish question – he was supposed to be there to support her, however she needed him to do that, and instead he was sitting ramrod-straight against the back of the couch worrying about an impending hard-on.

There was nothing he could do about it, nothing he could say as the movie played, failing to elicit laughter from either of them. He let her lean on him, because that was what he was there for – figuratively and literally, apparently – and tried not to enjoy it too much.

When the movie ended, Jed resisted the urge to breathe a sigh of relief. An hour and twenty minutes had rarely gone by so slowly or so torturously. When Karen sat up straight and shut off the TV with the press of a button, he became hopeful that his half-hard cock would finally soften.

"Can I get you something, Jed? There's not much ready to eat, but I could maybe whip something up, and there are drinks in the fridge. I just realized that you brought me that coffee, and I haven't offered you a thing."

"Don't worry about it. And you're not cooking." He pulled his phone from his pocket. "I'll order something in – what do you like?"

"You don't have to do that. I—"

"You need to eat." He tried not to sound too domineering, but it was true, and no way was he going to let her lift a finger on his behalf.

She glanced toward the nearest window, as if thinking of the places beyond. "There's this Japanese place that has great noodles. Sakura Sake House." She frowned.

"Do you know the number?"

She recited it from memory, and he caught himself filing the fact that she liked Japanese food away for future use.

Hitting call, he attempted to wipe the information from his brain. Her favorite foods were none of his business because he wasn't romancing her. He told himself that over and over as he remembered the feel of her body leaning against his, curled on the couch.

When the food arrived, they ate together at the kitchen table. There were prints hanging there too, and a couple of them were Jed's work. He fought to stifle the sense of prideful pleasure that came from knowing she'd been admiring his work in her home all this time. It was foolish, anyway – after all, it was her work, too.

It was their work.

Laying down a pair of bamboo chopsticks, he met her eyes. "It's starting to get late." The sky was a dusky purple beyond the kitchen window. "I'm glad to keep you company, but I don't want to keep you up, either. You have to be exhausted."

She laid down her chopsticks, too. "I am tired. But I don't want you to go, Jed. Not unless you need to – or want to."

"Abby's closing up the shop tonight. I don't have anywhere else I need to be." He never did. Hot Ink was his life. Often, when he was away from the studio, he felt a little like a fish out of water. In Karen's presence, he felt like a fish caught in a riptide, swimming against a current that threatened to pull him into waters he knew he should avoid.

"Will you stay, Jed – for the night? If you want to, I mean."

Hell yes, he wanted to. A very selfish, very powerful part of him wanted to. "I don't know if that's a good idea." When she recoiled, it hurt physically to watch. "Not because I don't want to," he said, "because I do want to."

She looked at him like she didn't understand, and he couldn't blame her. "When you spent the other night at my place, it was amazing," he clarified. "So amazing I can't stop thinking about it. I can't spend the night with you without thinking of what happened then, and that doesn't seem right. I want to be here for you, but I don't want to give my own selfish desires a chance to fuck everything up."

To his surprise, one corner of her mouth twitched in a quick half-smile. "I don't expect you to stop thinking of the other night. I haven't stopped. When I said I wanted you to spend the night, I meant with me – in my bed."

His chest suddenly felt too tight for his speeding heart. *Jesus.* "I can't do that, Karen. You can't— I mean, after last time…"

He summoned all of his willpower and forced out the truth. "The next morning, I realized how selfish I'd been, bringing you back to my place. After I told you about Alice and saw the way you held back around me – the way you were worried about hurting my feelings – I knew what I'd done was wrong. You deserve to be with someone that's not like me. Someone you don't feel the need to tone down your happiness around."

There, it was all out – having said the words left him feeling as if a crushing weight had been lifted off his chest, leaving a flattened, hollow space in its wake. It was a strange sort of relief, but a relief none the less.

"You're trying not to hurt my feelings right now." She shot him a level look across the table.

What was he supposed to say to that?

"I am," he replied eventually, having decided on undiluted honesty, "but that's because you've just lost someone you loved. The pain is fresh, and I know what it feels like – I don't want to make it any worse for you. But it's been five years since I lost Alice. I've had time to heal as much as I can, and I am what I am. And you think I'm sad."

She frowned and stood suddenly, pushing back her chair. "I don't think you're sad. I think what happened to you is sad – there's a difference. I'm sorry if I offended you by trying to be sensitive, but I didn't know how to act. I can only imagine what it's like to lose a spouse, Jed. I was just trying to put myself in your shoes. I guess I did a crappy job, but are you really so upset with me that you don't want to do this anymore?" She waved a hand between them.

"I just think you deserve someone different. You're only twenty-five, and you're so full of life. Hell, that's the first thing people notice about you – how alive you are, how much of yourself you put into everything you do. I just don't like the idea of being this person that burdens you with my sad history and makes you second-guess yourself."

"Then we have something in common," she said in an uncharacteristically even tone.

His heart sank even though he knew he should be glad he'd finally gotten her to see things his way.

"I mean about me putting so much of myself into everything I do," she continued. "You're the same way."

She motioned toward the nearest wall. "You're passionate, Jed. You couldn't create art like this if you weren't. I don't see you as some walking embodiment of tragedy. I see you as you are – as someone with a lot left to give. I want to be the person who…"

She paused and took a deep breath. "I want to be with you, Jed. I wanted you for months before I knew you were a widower, and I still want you just as much as I did then." She took a step toward him. "More, even, after what happened the other night."

He remained in his chair, the top of it digging into his vertebrae as he sat, struck dumb. It was hard to think past the whirling storm her words had turned his thoughts into. He struggled for a response, but nothing came to mind. And then she obliterated his concentration when she leaned down, wrapped her arms around his neck and pressed her mouth to his.

There was so much force in her kiss that her lips would've crushed his if they hadn't been so soft. As it was, they exerted cock-stirring pressure, bringing him to life in a way he couldn't resist, couldn't regret. Pulling her into his lap, he kissed her back, slipping his tongue deep into her mouth.

"Let me show you where you'll be sleeping," she said when their lips parted minutes later.

He went to her bedroom with her and didn't have time to so much as glance at the prints hanging on the walls there before they were on the bed, tangled in each other's arms. The words she'd spoken in the kitchen still rang in his ears, filling his mind with disbelief and his body with a desire so potent that time seemed to stop as he stripped her clothing off of her, revealing all the perfectly milky skin he'd been remembering so vividly for the past two days.

The world started turning again when she slid her hands beneath the hem of his t-shirt and unbuckled his belt, pulling his jeans down and wrapping her hands around his shaft. He sucked in a breath and reached for her.

Before he could make contact, she slipped her other hand into his pushed-down jeans, cradling his balls. That combined with the way she moved her hand up and down, from the base to the head of his dick, was enough to make him swear. Fuck, it had been hard to resist her, hard to tell her he wasn't right for her. And now here he was, despite his efforts. He didn't regret it. Not yet.

Finally wrapping his arms around her again, he pulled her close and kissed her hard before pulling off his disheveled clothing and throwing it all aside. Sinking down onto the mattress and lying chest-to-chest with nothing between their skins sent shivers of memory and expectation down his spine. Remembering what they'd done two days ago while anticipating what was about to happen … it was a combination that made his heart speed and his head spin as he kissed her, keeping his lips firmly against hers as he rolled on top of her.

He hadn't meant to stop there, with his hips between her thighs and his cock pressing up against the slick folds between them. When he'd lowered himself onto her, his head had been filled with vivid notions of sliding down and pushing her legs farther apart with his hands, opening her wide enough that no part of her would be hidden from his mouth. But before he could move a muscle, she reached down and pressed a hand against each of his ass cheeks, curling her fingers and letting her nails bite.

He couldn't resist her pulling him in, insistent as she tightened her grip, breathing a sigh. Not when he could feel the heat and wetness of her pussy against the head of his dick. With a moan, he flexed his hips, pushing past her folds and into the tight embrace of her body.

In one split second, he noticed and reveled in everything – the pulsing hitch her internal muscles gave when he pushed in to the root, the way she gripped him even harder, nails digging into the crease between his ass cheeks and his thighs, making his skin sting, and the way she exhaled against him, her breath warming his shoulder. All of it was enough to push him instantly to the edge, but she was so irresistible that he was torn between the urges to come and to stay inside her forever.

She rolled her hips, pulling back a little and then sending him plunging deep into her. The motion sent the breath rushing out of his lungs and was almost enough to make him lose it completely, too. Instead, he clung to every last scrap of self-control he had and focused on the splay of her hair against the pillow.

There were a dozen different shades of red and brown, and as she moved, they rippled beneath the overhead light, changing. He studied the light and shadow, the brilliant reds, and even thought about how he'd translate the shades and texture into a tattoo. He stopped when he sensed himself pulling back from the edge, back into a state where it was safe to enjoy every blistering second spent inside her body, undistracted.

She kept rocking her hips as he thrust, gripping a fistful of sheet as they moved to the same rhythm. Even their breathing seemed to be in sync – she exhaled hard and fast, as he did, and the sounds of breath and breathlessness blended with the faint banging of the mattress against the headboard. The symphony sent bolts of heat down his spine and into his groin, but he craved more. He thrust harder and faster, until she lost her rhythm and arched beneath him instead, breathing several wordless cries and then his name.

His name. The sound of it on her lips had his balls tight against his body, his dick aching for release inside her. He kept rocking into her, refusing to ease his rhythm until she reached climax. She was close; that was evident in the way she kept arching and squeezed her eyes shut as her lips moved, soundless now.

Seconds later, she shattered the quiet with a cry that went through Jed like an arrow, hitting some feral place inside him. The headboard banged against the wall, loud enough that he was probably damaging the drywall. He didn't care. He kept going, his hipbones pushing hard into her soft flesh with each stroke as her body pulsed around his cock, tightening with every fierce contraction.

Her pleasure rippled through her body and through his, leaving him feeling briefly as if every fiber of his being had been charged with electricity, left tingling and waiting – aching – for something to shatter. And then his climax hit him with crushing force, sending the air rushing out of his lungs as he thrust balls-deep inside her.

After several moments of blinding bliss, he opened his eyes and gave them time to focus again, bringing her beautiful face back into clear sight. Her cheeks were flushed a vivid shade of pink that had crept down and spread across her chest, and her eyes seemed brighter, too.

Withdrawing from between her thighs, he pressed his mouth to hers and let the heat of her lips soften the transition from inside her body to regular existence.

* * * * *

The water was scalding hot. It almost burnt her as it rushed over her body, but she was already red where a deep blush had spread beneath the surface of her skin as she and Jed had made love. She stood under the overhead spray, waiting for the color to fade from her skin and the fog of near-panic to lift from her mind.

The bliss of being tangled up with Jed had dominated her consciousness while they'd been in bed. But it had faded when she'd risen from the twisted sheets, swinging her legs over the edge. By the time her toes had brushed the carpet, a strange weight had slipped onto her shoulders, dispelling the satisfaction. The uncomfortable feeling had nothing to do with Jed – no, it had hit her when a little stuffed dog sitting on top of her dresser had caught her eye.

She'd bought it in the winery gift shop on Saturday, when she'd been there with her grandmother. It was supposed to be a gift for her cousin's three year old daughter – the kid was going through a puppy-obsession phase, and Karen had picked it up for her on a whim, meaning to mail it to her later. Now, even the memory of the little dog sent something sharp and searing through the center of Karen's being.

Was this the grief finally hitting her? She braced herself with a hand against the shower wall, her fingertips settling into the grooves between tiles. As she breathed a deep, shuddering breath, the next day's task of selecting flowers for the funeral service seemed repellant, impossible and more important than ever. How could she do that – how could she make arrangements to bury someone she couldn't imagine being gone?

Her grandmother seemed to wait around every corner of her mind, until she tried to focus, tried to recall – that was when the realization hit her, sudden and crushing: she wouldn't see her again. The memories were all she had, last impressions that were bound to fade with time.

She kept forgetting, kept remembering, and it hurt a little more each time, as reality began to drill the unchangeable fact into her forgetful mind.

She didn't realize she was crying until her eyes stung. Tilting her head back, she let the hot water hit her face, instantly washing the tears away. Better to let them escape now than to have to hold them back in Jed's presence. How could she cry in front of him when he'd suffered the ultimate loss, the death of a spouse? What she was feeling hurt, but his pain had to have been so much greater.

Most of the hot water was gone by the time a knock sounded at the door.

She jumped a little, her fingers slipping against the slick wall tiles. "Jed?"

The faint screech of door hinges sounded, and through the foggy glass shower panel, she could detect the motion of the door opening a little. Jed's head showed as a dark spot through the frosty glass. "Are you all right, Karen?"

"I'm fine." Her voice came out surprisingly, pleasingly steady.

"You've been in the shower for a long time. Thought I'd make sure everything's okay."

She shut off the tepid water and took a moment to smooth her expression before sliding the shower door open. "Thanks. But I'm okay."

Jed's eyes went wide as she revealed herself, stepping out onto the bathmat. For several silent moments, he stared, dark eyes shining with apparent concern … and something more.

She reached for a towel hanging on a nearby hook and wrapped it around her body.

His gaze continued to linger, now on her shoulders. "You sure? If I did something to upset you, you can tell me. Or if it's about what you're going through, you know you can talk to me, right?" He seemed earnest as he stood in the doorway, one arm braced against the frame, and Karen's heart did a cartwheel as she met his eyes.

"I guess I'm just now starting to realize what *gone* means. But Jed… I don't feel right talking to you about it. Not when you've been through so much worse." Her pain was real, but the prospect of baring her heart to Jed made her feel somehow selfish. After all, she'd never expected to outlive her grandmother; however much she'd enjoyed Helen's company, she'd always known that this day would come eventually.

Jed, on the other hand, had lost the person he'd sworn to spend the rest of his life with.

He didn't say so, but it had to hurt him to witness her sadness, to try to comfort her. Didn't it?

* * * * *

Jed's heart fractured as he stood across from Karen, watching water streak down her face and over the graceful lines of her collarbones, eventually dampening the towel she'd wrapped tight around her body. Maybe she thought he didn't realize she'd been crying, but the redness and slight puffiness around the edges of her eyes had betrayed her to him as soon as she'd stepped out of the shower. Even now, he noticed a tear slipping from one corner of her eye; the beads of liquid dripping from her sopping hair didn't hide it.

"Talk to me, Karen. I can handle it. I wouldn't have offered if I couldn't."

It was a lie. In that moment, he'd have done anything for her, even if it would've meant agony for him. But it wouldn't; in fact, a part of him sensed that if he could help her make sense of her own grief, it might give his some kind of meaning. And that would be a comfort, however small.

She made the slightest movement, as if she meant to step off the bathmat and come to him. Her shoulders went rigid as she stopped herself, and a dent appeared in her lower lip.

He went to her instead, wrapping his arms around her waist and pulling her close. Her body was soft beneath the scant cover of the towel, and it conformed to his as he embraced her. He held her tight, even tighter than he'd meant to as the memory of her picking up the red teapot in his kitchen played inside his head, crystal-clear.

One of the reasons why the sight of her holding the teapot had unsettled him had been because the object – the physical token of his grief – had seemed so out of place in her hands. There was a certain kind of innocence about her; she projected an air of passion, the sort of fearless zeal for life that could only exist in someone whose world had never been turned upside down by life's unfairness. It grated to see that innocence tainted, to think of her spending the night in the hospital, the only family member there to watch someone she loved die.

He'd only pulled on his jeans, no shirt. Something hot and wet dampened his shoulder – hotter than the lukewarm water that soaked her hair. At least he'd convinced her she could cry in front of him. It was a double-edged sword, sending relief and bitter sympathy slicing through him. "You two were close, weren't you?" Mina had said so.

Karen nodded, raising her head and meeting his gaze for a second before looking down again. "I was closer to my grandmother than my own mother, honestly. Plus, my parents live in Scranton, and I don't have any brothers or sisters. We spent a lot of time together. She wasn't your average grandmother."

Her voice hitched, but she took a deep breath and continued. "We did all kinds of things together. And at least one night a week, we'd order in, crack open a bottle of wine and stream a movie, usually after one of my photo shoots."

"Sorry," Jed said, knowing the word fell flat despite the fact that he meant it.

"She was my grandmother. I knew this would happen eventually. I guess I just didn't think it'd be so soon. She wasn't even seventy."

The fact that Karen's grandmother had only been in her sixties reminded Jed of Karen's youth, and his stomach clenched up into a hard ball when he thought of her sitting by a hospital deathbed. At least she'd had Mina, then. Now, she had him. And he'd been through it all; he understood. For the first time, he felt like he actually had something to offer her.

CHAPTER 7

"I almost forgot to tell you," Karen said, pausing with her fork buried in a half-eaten slice of cheesecake. "In a week, I'm leaving for New York."

Jed sat still too, turning dark eyes upon her from the other side of her small kitchen table. "New York?"

Was it just her imagination, or did he look grim as he gripped his fork, waiting for her to explain?

"Just for a few days," she said as realization dawned on her. Had he thought she meant permanently? She explained about the contest she'd won, about the incredible opportunity she'd all but forgotten about in the wake of her grandmother's death.

It had been a week since then – the memorial services had come and gone, and she'd spent the days since in an odd haze of grief and gladness. Jed was to thank for the gladness; they'd been spending a lot of time together. For some reason, he'd seemed to warm up to the idea of them being together after the first night he'd spent in her apartment, on the day he'd brought her coffee and offered her a shoulder to cry on.

"Sounds like it'll be great for your career." He carved a bite from the slice of homemade cheesecake Karen had baked for them to share. She'd done it as a small way to thank him for all the selfless support he'd shown her over the past week, and because the dessert had provided the perfect excuse to invite him over.

"It will be. Or at least, I hope so. Marc St. Pierre is a really respected designer in the bridal fashion industry. And the catalogs..." She didn't quite manage to suppress a sigh. "They're gorgeous. I can't believe my photographs are going to be in one."

"I can believe it." Jed stared at her over his coffee mug. "Your photos are amazing, Karen. I know you're shooting full-time now, but you still don't give yourself enough credit. I've been telling you for a while now that you're not charging me enough for the tattoo portraits. Every time you hand me an envelope full of prints, I feel like I'm stealing from you." He motioned at the wall, where half a dozen colorless prints hung in black frames. "You're an artist."

She hid a goofy grin with an especially large bite of cheesecake. When Jed complimented her, it always left her feeling as if there wasn't enough oxygen in the air. They'd made love nearly a dozen times now – the three nights he'd spent in her apartment had been especially intense – but she still found herself breaking out in embarrassing blushes and grins sometimes. "Thanks."

For some reason, when they embraced after finishing their dessert, he held her especially tight.

* * * * *

Jed carried the box down the stairs, through Hot Ink and out to his car, ignoring the way its corners dug into the insides of his arms, leaving red impressions on the little bits and pieces of uninked skin that showed through. It was the last one – for today. When he got it to the big house, where he had storage – an actual attic – he'd place it carefully there.

He'd still own Alice's teapot, dish towels and assorted other favorite household items, but he wouldn't display them, wouldn't section off special places in kitchen cupboards and drawers for them, allowing the air in those places to grow stale. He didn't use them, so there was no point – he didn't need Alice's things to remember Alice. She was in his heart and in his skin – those things would be enough.

After hefting the box into the back seat of his Charger, he felt oddly light, and not because he'd just put down a physical burden. Maybe he should've done this a long time ago.

Before slipping behind the wheel, he sent Karen a quick text, letting her know he was on his way over. Fifteen minutes later, he was idling at the curb in front of her apartment building. He went to the door and helped her carry her bags down the stairs and load them into the trunk. "Excited?" he teased as he pulled back out onto the street.

She smiled, her eyes bright as she shot him a sideways glance. "Maybe a little."

This had been his idea – for them to spend the night in the house he owned in North Side, in the Allegheny

West neighborhood. In the morning, he'd drop her off at the airport.

"Wow, this place is gorgeous. I had no idea you owned a house like this, Jed." She stepped out of the car and stood looking up at the Victorian brick structure, her lips slightly cracked.

"It's only been mine for a few years. Inherited it from a great aunt."

He hadn't known what to do with it at first. The house was old — nineteenth century — but his great aunt had kept it in excellent repair. After her death, he'd carefully maintained the place, sometimes coming over on his days off to take care of routine maintenance and make any needed small repairs. He'd paid the taxes on it, too. But that was it. He'd inherited the place a year after Alice's death, and the idea of moving in, of taking up residence alone in a big house she would've loved, had been incomprehensible then, with the loss so fresh.

He unlocked the front door and helped Karen carry her bags inside. "I thought you'd like it, after what you said about historical buildings that day in the studio when I caught you watching that ghost hunting show."

She grinned. "You weren't teasing me about this place being haunted, were you?"

His great aunt — who'd never balked at the notion of lingering spirits like he did — had said a few times that she thought there might be a spirit in the house. Harmless and only occasionally sensed, but there. He'd mentioned his aunt's claim to Karen on a whim, teasing her, and had immediately feared that he'd hurt her. Mentioning ghost stories so soon after her grandmother's death ... he'd cringed as he'd waited for her reaction. He didn't believe in that stuff, but for someone who did...

But she'd seemed interested, even delighted.

"My great aunt said she thought it might be. I've never seen anything. Don't know if she ever did either, for that matter."

"Well, you never know," she said, walking a circuit of the foyer and drifting toward the living area. "Have you ever spent the night here?"

"Not since I was a kid." He'd always returned to his apartment after spending time taking care of the house. He'd never had any desire to stay overnight before, but this – with Karen – seemed right. She was obviously getting a kick out of the historical house. It made him happy to see her so excited, running a hand reverently over a hand-carved bannister at the foot of the staircase, then inspecting an empty curio cabinet that stood in one corner of the living room.

"Are you ever going to move in?" she asked. "Or do you plan to sell it?"

He shook his head. "I wouldn't feel right selling this place. My great aunt loved the house so much – I know she wanted it to stay in the family." He didn't believe in ghosts, but he believed in honoring the memories of the dead when possible. "At first I couldn't imagine myself living here. But lately, I've been thinking the time may be right for a change."

"This place is so much bigger than your apartment." She tipped back her head, toward a high ceiling skirted by original crown molding.

He nodded, though it wasn't like he needed the space. The move he was contemplating was more about moving on. No more stagnating in his apartment just because he'd once shared it with Alice. No more leaving her things on display, untouched. Those old habits couldn't bring her back, so what was the point?

The apartment, the detritus of their long-vanished domestic life together … those things had rekindled his grief a dozen times a day, and in a way, keeping the fire alive had felt like loyalty. But deep down, he knew that was a lie, that it was exactly the opposite of what Alice would have wanted for him.

He gave Karen a tour, pointing out the house's original features and supplementing the architectural facts with what scraps of the place's history he could remember from his great aunt. Karen smiled and nodded and touched things carefully, like she was afraid she'd break something. Eventually he led her upstairs, to a hall lined with bedroom doors.

"I thought we could spend the night in this one," he said, opening the door to the master bedroom. "It still has a bed, and I brought some clean sheets."

Only some of his great aunt's furniture was still present in the house. She'd given him her home, but had left some of the furniture to other relatives. What was left would do, for now – for the night.

They made the bed together, layering linens and a comforter he'd picked up the day before. When that was done he wrapped his arms around her and pulled her down onto it, slipping a hand beneath her shirt and pushing it up, eventually pulling it over her head. After tossing her bra onto the hardwood floor, he cradled her breasts in his hands, squeezing as her nipples pricked against his palms, warm and hard.

He lowered his head, brushed the swell of one breast with his lips and closed his them around her nipple, drawing it deep into his mouth as he pressed a hand to the small of her back, liking the feel of her arching into him, her spine bowing beneath his fingers. He teased the stiff tip of her breast with tongue and teeth until she was writhing against him, breathing hard.

Unzipping the fly of her jeans, he dipped his fingers into her panties and found her clit. He rubbed it, letting friction warm his fingertips, until she came, her ragged breaths rushing through his hair and sending a frisson down his spine. Straightening, he raised his head and allowed his gaze to linger on her face, memorizing the auburn spread of her lashes fanned against the soft skin beneath her eyes.

Moments later she was fumbling with his belt buckle, loosening his jeans and raking her fingertips over his chest, beneath his shirt. He let her struggle with his clothing for a few moments, her nails scraping over the surface of his skin and making it pebble. Then he helped her, stripping off his things before divesting her of her jeans and panties.

He was guiding his hard cock into her before he knew it, pressing the head against her wet skin and pushing past her folds, into heat and pressure. She wrapped her legs around him, drawing him in and sighing when he sank all the way to the root of his dick, his hips flat against her body.

The bed was old but solid. It didn't make a sound as he fucked her with deliberate force, liking the way she clung tighter to him with each stroke. There was only the sound of rustling sheets and her breath, rushing through her parted lips.

By the time she arched against the bed with an internal tremor, the sheets were as hot as their bodies, impervious to the room's cool temperature. He drove her hard down into them, pushing her climax as far as he could. She was stronger than he'd realized – his ribs ached a little in the grip of her thighs, and the pressure there matched the ache in his balls, urging him to come inside her.

He held out until she relaxed beneath him, her body suddenly soft and recovering from a wrenching peak that had stolen her breath and weakened her muscles. And then he held out some more, not wanting it to be over. Taking it slow, he resolved to go softly until he felt her legs wrapped tightly around his waist again, or maybe her fingernails digging into his back. Then he'd give her a third orgasm, leave her breathless all over again.

He'd go until the lure of finishing was stronger than the appeal of making what they were doing last. Because this was the last time they'd sleep together before she left for New York, and he knew the opportunity she'd earned there would broaden her horizons, show her the world that was waiting outside of Pittsburgh for someone of her skill set and tenacity. And if that world snared her heart, he couldn't hold her back.

He'd just learned to let lost love go. What if the experience had been training, a test? It had taken him five years to fully come to terms with the fact that Alice was gone, and he might lose Karen in the span of a few days.

* * * * *

Natasha moved with a practiced grace, all long, slender limbs and cascading white silk, exactly the kind of model Karen was used to seeing in Marc St. Pierre bridal catalogs. She wore a lace stole over her shoulders and held a bouquet of deep red roses and white lilies – the effect was striking, especially in contrast to her long sable hair, which had been carefully styled, but left unbound. The winter bride look was gorgeous, and it would appear in the catalogs a few months from now, photographed by Karen. She got crazy, happy butterflies in her stomach just thinking about it.

Still, as she captured a shot that highlighted the graceful curve of Natasha's shoulder and showed off the back of the gown, she thought of Mina in her wedding dress – a real one, for a real bride. There had been a certain charm, a certain thrill found in taking those photos, knowing she was capturing a beautiful moment in a beautiful life.

As exciting as it was to photograph a real New York fashion model in a real designer dress, the elaborate set was just an imitation of real life, and Karen was aware of that – aware of the fact that her job was to make it all look like a glamourized version of reality to the brides who'd open the Marc St. Pierre winter lookbook.

After Karen finished photographing Natasha alone, a groom walked onto the set. He was classically handsome with neat, dark hair and a trim build showcased by a perfectly-tailored tuxedo. He posed with a natural grace too, and together, he and Natasha looked beautiful.

Photographing them wasn't like photographing a real bride and groom, though. The photos were about showing off the clothing, not the couple or their love, which of course didn't exist. Karen kept that in mind, capturing images that would display the beautiful wedding wear to full advantage. The models were just perfect – just conventional – enough that they'd fade into the background, living canvases for high-end style.

Karen couldn't help but think of the people she photographed most often back in Pittsburgh – the friends, the Hot Ink clients and the real-life bride and grooms – so many of whom had turned their bodies into canvases for artwork by artists like Jed and Eric.

The Marc St. Pierre winter lookbook would be a one-time publication, the fashions within fleeting. Taking the photos was a killer career opportunity, but ultimately, the images would find their way into recycling bins and garbage cans. No one would cherish them forever.

The realization stood in contrast to the highly-personal nature of the portrait sessions she often conducted back home. But hey, at least no one was peeing in the corner of the studio. Photographing fashion models might not be as meaningful as photographing tattoos or real-life people celebrating real-life occasions, but it was a heck of a lot better than trying to capture decent images of a spastic greyhound.

There were even assistants – photographer's assistants, wardrobe assistants, the list went on – ready to primp and perfect every last little detail. They worked attentively, leaving Karen to focus on what she loved – taking photos. It definitely wouldn't be hard to get used to that.

* * * * *

Jed's phone rang just as he was exiting his half-booth. He pulled the door shut behind himself as he motioned for Abby to shut off the shop's 'open' sign. "Hey," he said, a wave of heat and awareness sweeping over his skin as he braced himself for the sound of Karen's voice.

"Hey," she replied from the other end of the connection, her tone pleasant, upbeat.

"How's New York?" She'd texted him a few times to let him know everything was going well, but this was the first time they'd spoken. It hadn't been long – today was day two of a three day trip, but he'd been constantly aware of her absence.

"It's great, Jed. The shoot today was amazing. I had assistants! Not that anybody peed on anything in the studio, but it was nice having them around anyway."

"I bet."

He could practically hear her grinning, and it made him smile too as he leaned against the wall. Abby kept glancing his way, looking quizzical, but there was no one else in the shop, so he made no effort to seek out privacy. "You ready to fly home tomorrow, or has the Big Apple won you over?"

"Actually, that's why I called – I'm not going to be coming home tomorrow."

Jesus. He'd only been teasing. His heart slammed against his chest, then slowed, succumbing to a heavy certainty. It was like his brain was telling his heart *I told you so.* "Everything all right?" He managed to think rationally enough to ask, to make sure she wasn't stranded or hurt somehow.

"Yeah, everything's great. I managed to change my scheduled flight, and I'm paying the difference plus the cost of another night in the hotel out of my own pocket. It'll be worth the money – I want another day to see the city."

"You're only staying one extra night?"

"That's right. I made friends with another photographer today – one who shoots regularly for Marc St. Pierre – and she invited me to spend the day with her tomorrow."

"Sounds fun." His shock ebbed, but a deep-seated sense of caution remained. "What are you two going to do?"

"We're stopping by her studio, going out to lunch and to a really cool framing place in SoHo. I'm going to buy a nice frame to use for a wedding portrait of Mina and Eric – it'll be a gift." She sighed. "This place does *museum* quality framing jobs, Jed. I don't have a print with me, of course, so I'll just be buying an empty frame, but it should still be amazing."

Despite the heavy feeling in the pit of his chest, he couldn't help but smile a little over her passion for photo frame shopping, of all things. "Hope you have a good time. Still need a ride home from the airport day after tomorrow?"

"Only if it won't be too much trouble for you. If you'll be with a client, I can see if Mina's free, or take a cab home."

"Don't worry about it. I'll be there. What time does your flight come in?"

"Six-thirty."

"I'll see you then."

"Thanks. I'd be lying if I said I wasn't glad you'll be picking me up. I miss you, you know." A breathy sound came from her end of the connection, and it sent a slow frisson creeping down Jed's spine.

"Yeah. Spending the night in that big haunted house just isn't the same without you."

"You slept there alone?" She sounded genuinely surprised.

"Last night. Going back tonight, too."

"Wow, you're brave."

"Just facing my fears."

She laughed, but he hadn't been joking. Spending the night alone in the place in Allegheny West had very much been about facing ghosts. Not the kind that walked through walls and whispered in your ear, but the ones in his head.

* * * * *

Karen reached out and touched one finger gently to the side of a thick picture frame, tracing the curve of a golden lily with the tip of one finger. Her grandmother would love everything about it – the way the burnished gold made it look antique, the way the ornate carvings scrolled from corner to corner in the shapes of dozens of lilies. She—

Realization hit Karen like an arrow to the heart, sharp and piercing. Her grandmother *would have* loved the picture frame. She lowered her hand and moved on, searching for something that would suit Mina and Eric's style.

"These are gorgeous," said Miranda, the photographer Karen had hit it off with the day before. "Very modern, but still unique, you know?"

Karen nodded. "I like this one." She reached out and touched silver, thinking of Jed. How many times had he been hit by those sharp little arrows, those split second realizations that reminded you of a sickening truth you'd somehow forgotten?

He was strong, though, and she endeavored to be strong too as she glanced back at the lily frame and attempted to appreciate it for what it was, for what her grandmother would have liked about it. She didn't want to stop thinking about her just because it hurt – truly forgetting her would be the worst tragedy of all, something she wouldn't be able to forgive herself for.

"It's nice." Miranda eyed the frame, giving it an appreciative nod. "Think the bride-to-be would like it?"

In the end, Karen decided that yes, Mina would like it. A salesperson carried it to the register, wrapped it carefully and surrendered the bag after a swipe of Karen's credit card.

Moments later, Karen and Miranda were out the door, on their way to a place Miranda promised Karen she'd love.

Inside one of Miranda's favorite restaurants near the frame gallery, Karen placed her shopping bag beneath the table.

"So," Miranda eventually said, smiling over a bowl of soup, "when are you coming back to New York?

"I don't know," Karen said, a little wave of surprise rippling over the surface of her mind as she paused with a spoonful of French onion halfway to her mouth. "I don't have any plans to return right now, why?"

"You want to be a fashion photographer, don't you? That's why you entered the contest. Well, it's not like you're going to make a name for yourself shooting fashion in Pittsburgh. That'd be like trying to fish in the desert – pointless."

Karen mulled the analogy over and nodded. The Steel City was full of bridges, not runways. The fashion work was in New York. Everyone knew that.

"So, you've got talent," Miranda continued. "But talented photographers are a dime a dozen. More importantly, you've got opportunity – give it a few months, and you'll have Marc St. Pierre tear sheets. It's tough to make it in fashion, in New York – but you know that. Point is, play your cards right and you'll be a fresh – dare I say *exciting* – new arrival on the fashion scene instead of just another hopeful with a camera."

"I guess I hadn't looked at it that way – I hadn't considered *moving* here."

"Why not?"

Karen dipped her spoon back into her bowl, stirring its steaming contents as she bit down on her inner lip.

"Look," Miranda said, "I grew up in a wide spot in the road in Georgia. I *know* how daunting the idea of striking out on your own here can be. But Marc St. Pierre – hell, I felt like I'd just discovered the Holy Grail the first time I booked a shoot with them. And it took me a long time to work my way up to landing that job. I spent years sharing an apartment the size of a postage stamp with two other women and eating peanut butter sandwiches most days."

Karen finally lifted a spoonful of the soup to her mouth. As it slid down her throat, spicy and hot, she tried to imagine living in the city, devoting her life to shooting gazelle-like models in designer clothing – or at least, trying to land jobs where she could do just that.

"What I'm really trying to say is that if you do want to give it a real try here, I can help. You saw my studio – it doesn't come cheap. I rent it out to other photographers on a fairly regular basis to help recoup the cost. If you move here, we can negotiate a rental agreement so that you'll have a place to shoot indoors when needed, right off the bat. It wouldn't be free, but I wouldn't price-gouge you, either." She grinned broadly from across the table. "I'd even make sure you don't get stuck on an all peanut butter diet."

Karen's imagination soared at the thought of shooting inside Miranda's studio on a regular basis. It was no wonder she rented it out – it was a dream facility in the city, with its amazing location, wide-open space, high ceiling and abundant natural lighting provided by huge windows that showcased the Manhattan skyline. And it was stocked with top of the line equipment – stuff that Karen's own supplies back in Pittsburgh paled in comparison to.

"It's your decision, obviously," Miranda said, "and I've made my offer, so I won't pressure you anymore. But I really think you owe it to yourself to make the most of the opportunity you've been granted and give New York a try."

* * * * *

Jed's heart beat just a little too quickly as he guided the Charger down a nighttime street, leaving the airport behind. When Karen had emerged into the baggage claim area, she'd embraced him, and when they'd slipped into the car together, she'd given him a sultry smile that had thrown him into the grip of memories of their night together in the Allegheny West house.

Now he drove, expectation tingling in his veins as a sense of apprehension weighed him down. Karen had been quiet since they'd entered the car – a rarity, for her. "How was the rest of your trip?"

She beamed. "Great. I found the perfect frame for Mina and Eric. It's in my suitcase, but I'll show you when we get to my place."

When they arrived at her apartment, she invited him in first thing, then embraced him again before pulling a silver picture frame out of her luggage.

"Looks great," he said, shifting his weight from one foot to the other.

She set it on the kitchen table, reverently re-wrapping it in several layers of paper. "There's something I want to talk to you about, Jed," she said when she faced him again.

A weight tumbled from somewhere in his throat to the pit of his gut as a sense of the inevitable settled over him. "Okay. What is it?" He could handle this – he had to. She deserved New York; she deserved the best of everything, including the best possible chance for her career.

CHAPTER 8

"I want you to tattoo me."

It took a few moments for her words to settle in. "You do?" He searched her face, meeting her unblinking eyes and examining them for any trace of a joke, any evidence that he'd misheard.

"Yes." She stood with her hands clasped together, her eyes wide. "Will you?"

"Of course." A fierce wave of emotion flashed through him at the thought of his gloved hands against her uninked skin, his needle poised to leave a permanent mark.

She breathed a sigh, her shoulders relaxing. "Oh, good. I thought you'd laugh at me."

"Why would I?"

"Because, you know, I'm afraid of needles, and I've always said there was no way I could get a tattoo."

He knew that, of course, and the knowledge only made it that much more gratifying that she apparently trusted him to tattoo her. "I'm not going to laugh. What made you change your mind?"

"I want a tattoo to honor my grandmother. When I was in that frame gallery in SoHo, I found a frame she would've loved. It had lilies worked into the design – stargazer lilies were her favorite flower. She loved them. She used to pick up a little bunch from the florist every week and display them in a vase in her kitchen, and I would always give her a huge bouquet of them on her birthday."

"So you want a tattoo of those flowers?"

She nodded. "I thought of it a little while after I left the frame place. I know that was only yesterday, but I'm sure I want it." She exhaled, eyes flashing. "Even if that means I have to voluntarily come into contact with a needle."

"And you need a design?"

She nodded again.

"Do you have a piece of paper and a pencil I can use?"

"Yeah." She retrieved both items and surrendered them, looking curious.

"Can you bring up a picture of a stargazer lily on your phone?"

"Sure." She brought one up, and he took the phone, studied the image for a few seconds and then laid the device on the table where he could see the screen easily.

"Where do you want the tattoo?"

"On my shoulder. Here." She crossed her left arm over her body and touched her fingertips to her back, running them over the area just above her shoulder blade.

"Okay. Now explain to me what you have in mind for the design."

As she spoke, he sketched, doing his best to translate what she was describing into an illustration. Two lilies and a delicate swirling design behind them, darker than the flower petals, which would be carefully shaded in tones of pink and white. For now, he used the flat side of his pencil to color in shades of grey where the pink would go.

Karen watched with a bright smile as he used the tip of the pencil to add dots to the petals, a freckling pattern like the one belonging to the real-life flower displayed by her phone.

"That looks amazing," she said when he was done. "Like I imagined, only even better."

"It's just a rough sketch. I can take this home and draw up something neater."

"Really? Thank you. I love it."

"We can do the tattoo whenever you're ready."

"I'm as ready as I'm ever going to be. Whenever you have time will be fine."

"Tomorrow night, if you're sure."

She nodded. "Thank you. And ... how much?"

He did laugh then – he couldn't help it. "I'm not charging you anything."

"I don't expect you to do it for free. I'll pay whatever you'd charge any other client."

He shook his head. "No way. It'll be a gift."

Maybe she sensed his resolve, because she nodded, thanking him again.

And then, with the preliminary sketch lying on the table before him, there was nothing to do but address what had been eating away at him for over a week. "Karen, did your trip change how you view your career – do you plan to go back to New York?"

She raised her gaze from the sketch, blinking. "I'm sure I'll return at some point."

"I mean, do you plan to move there to pursue your photography?"

Her eyes widened, but she shook her head. "No, why?"

"I'm no photographer, but I know New York is where all that stuff happens with fashion. I figured if models go there to try to make it big, photographers must too, right? After getting a break with a famous designer there, I thought you might decide to stick around for any other opportunities that might bring."

"New York definitely supplies the lifeblood of the country's fashion industry. And Miranda, the photographer I spent yesterday with, did offer to rent me partial use of her studio if I move to the city."

He nodded, resignation stiffening the bones and muscles in his neck, making the motion difficult. What she was saying made sense – why was it so hard to accept, especially when he'd been expecting it? "Pittsburgh is so small compared to New York. When you told me you won that contest, I figured…"

His voice faded, betraying him as he remembered her legs wrapped around his waist, her nails digging into his back. Maybe he could still see her even if she moved to New York.

Hell, no, that was just wishful thinking. The drive was a good seven hours, not even counting city traffic. Way too long to work, way too much to ask. And Pittsburgh, where he'd built Hot Ink from the ground up, was his home, for good. The idea of a long-distance relationship was ridiculous, and a sinking part of him knew it.

"You thought I'd want to stay in New York?" She arched a brow. "Then this will sound crazy, but... Jed, I don't want to be a fashion photographer. I realized that when I was shooting for Marc St. Pierre."

"You don't want to be a fashion photographer?" The words felt alien on the tip of his tongue, false. Was his disappointment so obvious that she was lying to him, denying her dream to try to spare his feelings? The thought made his head ache as a wave of faint nausea washed over him.

"I know what you must be thinking. I almost feel bad saying it, after being granted such an awesome opportunity. I enjoyed the shoot and I'll be showing the catalog off every chance I get when it comes out this winter, but I'm just not interested in pursuing fashion photography as a career. I want to focus on other areas."

"Other areas?" He looked around at the many black and whites hanging on her apartment walls, his gaze lingering on the beautiful photographs of his work. Her tattoo portraits were amazing, and they may have given her the boost she needed to go full-time with her photography, but tattoo photography alone couldn't sustain a career. Surely she realized that.

"Shooting for Marc St. Pierre was fun, but it's just so different than what I really love shooting – people, their stories, their tattoos, the important moments in their lives... I love taking photos that people will cherish or admire for the rest of their lives, not advertisements that will be thrown out after a few weeks. Does that make any sense?"

He nodded, slowly. "Still, couldn't you continue to take the sort of photos you love most on the side, in addition to fashion photography?" He was no expert, but advertisements sounded a hell of a lot more lucrative than portrait and personal photography.

"I guess. I mean, that's basically what I'm doing now – I've done commercial shoots for quite a few businesses here in Pittsburgh. But if I relocated to New York to pursue fashion photography… I think it would be sink or swim, you know?

"It's a hard business to make it in, and a hard city to afford. Miranda's studio is state of the art, but I'd have to work my butt off to have a chance at being able to afford the rent, not to mention my living expenses. And frankly, I don't want to do that. I don't want to struggle for a chance to make it in an industry my heart isn't really in. I like what I have here – I want to continue to grow my business in Pittsburgh, and spend as much time as possible on the projects that are meaningful to me."

"Are you sure?" He had to ask – had to. Because what she was saying was almost too good to be true, and not making sure it was really, truly what she wanted most would've been selfish.

She laughed softly. "You almost sound like you want to get rid of me, Jed. You're not going to force me onto a one-way flight back to New York, are you?"

"No. I just need to make sure that you're telling me the truth – that you're not just saying all this because we've been seeing each other." It seemed kind of egotistical to say it out loud, but if the attraction she felt to him was anything like what he felt for her … well, it was a powerful fucking thing.

She looked directly into his eyes, unblinking. "Pittsburgh – my life and my work here – is really what I want. I'm not being dishonest. Not even a little bit. And maybe if we'd been seeing each other a little longer, you'd know me well enough to realize that if I was lying, I'd be blushing really badly right now. I don't have a poker face, Jed, so I usually don't even try to deceive people." She grinned.

He drummed his fingertips on the table, mulling the situation over, mentally exploring every facet as best he could. He wanted to stand up and sweep her right off her feet, but only if he wouldn't be pulling her future out from under her by doing so. "Okay." What she'd said was pretty thorough, and if that was what she wanted, who was he to tell her what to do?

"Okay as in you're not going to try to force me into fashion photography?" Her grin stretched a little wider. "Okay as in we can pick up where we left off before I went to New York, and you'll stop looking like you're waiting for me to give you a good, sharp kick in the shin?"

His lips twitched at the corners, bowing to an involuntary smile. "Is that what I look like?"

"Pretty much. But for the record, I've never seen someone look so sexy while anticipating being hurt."

"Thanks." He stood, reaching for her, placing his hands on her hips and pulling her close.

"Did you really think I was going to want to stay in New York? For good?" She leaned into him, her breath warming his chest, even through his t-shirt.

"Yeah." He wrapped his arms around her waist. "How was I supposed to know you're the one woman in the world who'd rather photograph tattoos in Pittsburgh than designer wedding dresses in New York?"

He could still hardly believe it. Maybe he was just being stupid – Karen wasn't the average woman; he'd already known that. She was the first woman he'd been genuinely interested in since Alice, the first woman who'd inspired him to look to the future instead of the past.

She tipped her head, her eyes flickering toward the back wall, which bore at least a dozen different framed prints. "The pictures should've been a clue."

"Guess you could say I was distracted by other things whenever I was in here." He ran a hand down her back, letting his fingertips skim the little valley above her hips before he reached below and grasped one round, perfect half of her ass.

She arched against him, slipping her arms around his sides and tipping her head back to look up at him. "You *feel* distracted right now."

Yeah, he did – his dick was hard, pressing against the front of his jeans, against her belly. Expectation rippled through his veins like an electric current as he flexed his hips, letting his stiffness press a little harder against her, swelling further beneath the brief friction.

She sucked in a hard breath, then exhaled, letting it rush out against his ear. It tickled, and heat blazed a trail down his spine and into his groin. "Missed you," she whispered.

He swept her off her feet, just as he'd imagined seconds ago. Briefly, he held her, and then he lowered her onto the kitchen table, barely pausing before popping her jeans button through its hole and making short work of the zipper.

She raised her hips, making it easy for him to shimmy the pants down over her thighs, eventually pulling them free and tossing them aside.

Her panties were wet. A faint shadow of dampness was visible just below her mound, beneath the little bump of her clit. The sight of it made his dick throb and sent a wave of regret washing through him. Peeling off her panties as quickly as he could, he discarded them, afterward sliding his hands up the insides of her thighs and spreading them apart.

She looked, smelled and tasted just like he'd remembered so vividly while she'd been gone. The flavor of her slick skin sparked a burst of bone-deep want inside him, and he applied his tongue to the small swell of her clit with all the fervor he'd kept bottled up during the past several days. When she sighed and a wave of motion raced through her hips, making them buck against the table top, he gripped her thighs more firmly and refused to relent.

She'd missed him. She'd said so, and he could tell it was true as he ran the tip of his tongue over the seam of her pussy, delving inside. She said his name, the single syllable shattered by several hitching breaths. When he lifted his gaze briefly, he could see that her knuckles were white, her fingers hooked over the edge of the table top.

He'd missed her too, bad. When he'd lain down in bed at the Allegheny West house, thoughts of her had come to him in the dark. For short seconds, he'd almost tasted her, almost smelled the sweet musk of her skin. And a part of him had begun to mourn the loss he'd been anticipating – the loss of true affection and true pleasure so recently rediscovered.

It was amazing, really, that he'd been wrong. He couldn't fuck things up now, couldn't slide back into assuming and fearing and thinking he saw her future more clearly than she did. If the past had taught him anything, it was that life was full of twists and turns you just couldn't see coming. Maybe they weren't all bad.

"Ahh!" She stopped breathing his name, stopped moving against the table. She was stock-still for a few moments, until a tremor shot through her, making her muscles shift and tighten beneath his hands. He stroked her clit with his tongue, unyielding as he felt the tension in her body rise to a fever-pitch. His heart raced, beating in time with an answering throb that tortured him below the belt.

She cried out when her hips began to move again, rising and falling as much as they could with him holding her steady. He let her sounds drive him on, more breath than voice. His cock was so hard against his jeans it hurt, but when she was quiet, he rose.

She leaned forward, reaching for him, and pulled him close with her arms wrapped around his waist and her temple against his heart. "Want to take this back to the bedroom?" she asked after a silent minute, "or..." She tucked a thumb into the waistband of his jeans, looking up at him with slightly hazy eyes.

He slipped a hand behind her head, cradling the curve of her skull and sweeping a lock of hair out of her eyes. "I can't stay."

She blinked. "You can't?"

He shook his head. "I've got some things I need to do. You'll see tomorrow."

"Okay." She eased back a little. "Is everything all right?"

"Yeah." He'd have to live with the agony of unsatisfied desire for the night, but he couldn't resist kissing her deeply, giving it a sharper edge. "We'll do your tattoo as soon as the shop closes tomorrow night, all right? That way we'll have the place to ourselves."

She nodded, and he picked up her jeans and panties, handing them to her before leaving. Outside, the night air cooled his skin by a few degrees but did nothing for his aching hard-on.

As he made his way to his car, he dialed Hot Ink's number. "You're still there – good," he said when Eric picked up. The studio was closing – Zoe was probably already gone, and he was lucky he'd caught Eric before he closed up for the night. "Would you mind staying a while longer? I need you to do something for me."

* * * * *

Karen slipped beneath the sheets, a dull ache present in the pit of her chest, just beside her heart. It sharpened when she thought of Jed, remembering the look in his eyes when he'd thought she was going to relocate her business and life to New York.

How could he have thought that, and how could she not have realized that the possibility had been eating away at him? The thought of him spending lonely nights in the Allegheny West house was triply-saddening when the revelation of his thoughts came into play. And still…

Excitement sizzled and crackled through her when she thought of the next night. The sketch Jed had drawn up for her tattoo was every bit as amazing as he was. She wanted something to remember her grandmother by, something as unfading as the impression Helen had left on her life. The ink would be just that, beauty that would live and die with her.

And she trusted Jed to make it beautiful. That was the other aspect of the tattoo that had her looking forward to the following night – being tattooed by Jed. The idea made her skin tingle and all her internal muscles draw up tight, much as they had an hour ago when she'd been perched on the edge of the kitchen table. Needles still set her teeth on edge, but if she was going to be tattooed – and she was determined to be – it was going to be by Jed.

He'd shown so much concern and selflessness when it came to her future; there was no one she'd trust more to mark her permanently.

* * * * *

Jed settled onto the bed, his right side aching as his left side met the sheets. The physical pain was dull, not enough to distract him from his real purpose in spending the night alone in the Allegheny West house again.

Memories of Alice sailed through the dark and across the surface of his mind, sending ripples and echoes of the past through his consciousness. Then came memories of Karen, and eventually both at once. Was it strange that he could think of Alice and Karen almost at the same time?

They both anchored his thoughts, tying him to memories that ran deep. Alice was like ivy clinging and blossoming in every nook and cranny of his memory; she'd been the center of his existence for over a decade, since he'd started dating her at nineteen, married her at twenty and lost her at thirty.

She was still with him, a presence in his mind, his heart, his skin. She was a part of who he was – how could he have lived out some of the most defining years of his life with her and that not be the case?

Losing her had been like losing a limb. He'd gone on without her – he'd had little choice – but his progression through life had been slowed, often painful and at times downright fucking awkward as he'd struggled to limp forward, always missing that absent part of himself.

There was no recovering a lost limb, and likewise, there was no replacing Alice, and no forgetting her. Which was exactly why he'd figured he'd never be serious with anyone else.

Over the years since Alice's death, he'd had a few encounters with other women. They'd been short-lived, disappointing and were half-shameful in retrospect. Nothing more than attempts at escape from reality, they'd all failed. After a while, he'd stopped paying attention to any woman who'd seemed interested, stopped giving a damn about anything except Hot Ink.

That, at least, had been a safe harbor for his passion, even after Alice's death. Hot Ink had been her dream too; they'd started the shop together with just him tattooing and her working reception during every open hour. She'd handled the accounting and many of the day-to-day business matters, and she'd been good at it.

During her dying months, she'd forced him to take little lessons from her, to learn to do it all himself. He clung to those tasks, cherishing the numbers, the tax forms

… everything she'd passed down to him, as unromantic as it all was.

Karen was not Alice, and not a replacement for her, by any means. No one could be that; love couldn't be replicated, and every relationship was unique. Karen and Alice weren't much alike, anyway. And still, he felt happier with Karen in his life than he'd been since before Alice's cancer diagnosis.

Being with Karen felt right, like new life had been blown into his lungs. Still, the feeling didn't dispel the pain of losing Alice. That fact was exactly what gave him confidence in what was growing between him and Karen. Karen wasn't a crutch, wasn't a distraction – she was much more than that. She was someone he could love without fooling himself, without abusing his feelings for her like a drug, using them to numb his negative emotions.

Alone in the otherwise empty house with the past and the future laid before him in his head, he let the realization wash over him, easing his mind enough that he noticed the ache in his side again.

* * * * *

"These colors are going to look great against your skin."

A wave of heat shimmered over the curve of Karen's shoulder as Jed passed his hand over the area, moistening her skin with cleansing alcohol. She raised her gaze to the wall of his half-booth, where a vase full of stargazer lilies rested. They'd been there when he'd welcomed her into the closed tattoo studio.

"Do you think so?" She'd chosen to have the lilies done in true-to-life shades of pink and white because that was what her grandmother's favorite flowers had looked like. She let her gaze wander over the living blossoms again, studying the play of light on their crisply-colored petals.

Her tattoo would look much like them when it was done; Jed was a master at using color, at creating tattoos that not only looked vibrant when finished, but were designed to stand the test of time, to look good years later. Clients came to him from places far beyond Pittsburgh for those reasons – she'd heard them say so, had seen them show off their older tattoos in the shop while returning for another.

"Yeah. The bright pink, the white and the black – your fair skin is the perfect canvas for this tattoo. I think you'll be happy with it."

She studied his reflection in the mirror that took up the booth's back wall, watching him as he stood bent over her shoulder, carefully preparing the area. "I know I'll be happy with it." She didn't feel the sense of trepidation she'd always imagined she would if she ever decided to be tattooed. She felt a calmness that remained as Jed applied a stencil to her skin.

"Made this earlier today," he said, and slowly spun her chair so that the mirror reflected her back. "What do you think?"

She peered over her shoulder at the purplish outline of two lilies and the swirling design behind them. "Looks great." It was just a silhouette, but it conveyed the same promise of beauty she'd sensed as she'd watched him draw the original sketch.

She sat still in the chair as he turned away and prepared his equipment, unpackaging needles, readying the inks and situating everything on a sterile tray. She'd watched him do this before and was familiar with the way he organized things. It was the actual tattooing that she'd preferred not to watch, thanks to the unnerving buzz of the needle.

"Ready?" He met her eyes in the mirror, apparently waiting for her to give her final approval.

Once, in this same shop, she'd sat with Mina, watching Eric tattoo her. She'd been talkative then, and clearly remembered having had no problem making conversation. Now, her own voice shrank away from her. "Yes," she said after a couple moments, carefully annunciating the simple word.

"Okay." He stood behind her, equipment in hand, clean and gleaming. In that moment, Karen understood why so many people called the machines tattoo guns – she felt almost as if she were waiting to be shot.

"Take a deep breath," he said, "I can give you a second. There's no rush."

She nodded, drew a deep breath and exhaled. "I'm ready," she said afterward. "I don't want to procrastinate like a baby. Just go ahead."

"All right. It's important that you hold still. If it gets to be too much and you need a break, just let me know. We'll do whatever you can handle comfortably. If you decide you want to break this tattoo up into more than one session, we can do that too."

"Okay." Inwardly, she resolved that she would make it through the entire tattoo in one session. She could do this. She'd summoned the nerve to admit to herself – and others – that she wasn't interested in being a fashion photographer, in fully exploiting an opportunity so many others would've killed to have. Admitting what she really wanted had been a relief, had left her feeling empowered. So did this. She wanted the tattoo, and she would face her fear of needles to have it.

CHAPTER 9

The first line of the tattoo blazed a stinging trail across her skin, as did the second. In some areas, the pain seemed deeper – almost an ache – while at other times, it was faint.

"You okay?" Jed asked after what had to only have been a minute or so, pressing a clean cloth gently against her shoulder.

When he lowered it, it was stained with black ink.

"Yeah." When she was in pain, talking seemed less appealing than usual. And she was afraid she'd move, afraid she'd mess up Jed's work of art. So she sat silently, focusing on the tattoo portraits on the wall – she'd taken them – which showcased some of Jed's best work.

She studied the lines and shading of the tattoos, remembering the photo sessions she'd captured the images during. She allowed her mind to wander back in time and tried not to think of needles.

It was kind of hard not to do, in a tattoo studio. She felt the piercing pressure of the needle in her flesh, burrowing beneath the surface and planting pain between the layers of her skin. And yet, she'd lost most of the original horror she'd felt at the idea of being tattooed. Now that she was actually facing her fear, the fear seemed smaller. It was a relief, and she sighed.

"Everything all right?" Jed paused, pressing the cloth to her shoulder again.

She nodded, and he went back to work.

It had been late when they'd started, after the end of Hot Ink's business hours, and it was well past midnight by the time they finished. They'd paused for some relatively short breaks, but Karen had made it through the entire tattoo. The lingering pain took a backseat to a sense of satisfaction, and she felt more accomplished than relieved.

"Ready to take a look?"

"Yes."

Though she'd known exactly what to expect, the reflection of her tattoo took her by surprise. The shades of pink, black and white knocked the air right out of her lungs in a little gasp, and she stood and moved closer to the mirror, studying everything, down to the little black dots that graced the lily petals. "Jed, this is perfect. I love it!"

She grinned at herself in the mirror, unable to help it. Her heart was beating a little faster at just the sight of the amazing tattoo. Maybe this was why people came back time and time again to be tattooed at Hot Ink.

He smiled too. "Glad you like it. Why don't you have a seat again while I get you bandaged up?"

He applied a protective ointment to her skin, coating the area in a light sheen before cutting a bandage and securing it. When he was done, she looked more like she'd been to the hospital than a tattoo studio, but she couldn't forget the beauty hidden by the gauze and medical tape, and her smile lingered.

Time seemed to speed by after that, minutes blurring into seconds as Jed cleaned up his work area and they climbed the stairs to his apartment. Nothing had been said about how they'd spend the rest of the night, but the air felt almost electric, and Karen's skin tingled, beneath the bandage and elsewhere. When Jed unlocked the door at the top of the steps, the apartment was just as she remembered it.

Mostly. She glanced toward the kitchen, where the absence of the red teapot was immediately apparent. The sight of the empty burner where it had rested sent a bittersweet pang through her chest, and she turned to Jed. It was only the second time she'd been in his apartment, and though it hadn't been that long ago, it was sort of staggering how much things had changed since then, for her and – she sensed – for him.

"This'll be my last night here," he said, pulling the door shut, "I'm moving most of my stuff over to the Allegheny West house tomorrow. Already rented a moving truck."

She nodded, her gaze wandering over their surroundings before returning to him. "Let's make it a good last night, then." She smiled, and it was a relief when he returned the expression. She knew so much more than she had when she'd first spent the night inside the apartment, and the knowledge burnt inside her, fueling hope that the sadness the place had known could somehow be sealed off by love, left in the past.

She had no delusions that he could forget the years he'd spent alone in the apartment above Hot Ink, or that he'd want to. But he'd clearly decided on change, and that made her want to breathe a sigh of relief.

The bedroom was exactly how she remembered it, and the bed was soft beneath her when he wrapped his arms around her and they sank down onto it, settling with her halfway in his lap.

She'd worn a strapless sundress, purposely having chosen something that would leave her shoulders bare for the tattooing process. He unzipped it in the back, baring her to the waist in one easy movement.

He sighed, his breath rushing hot against her ear and neck as he reached around her from behind and cradled her breasts. She hadn't worn a bra – one, because strapless bras were torture devices, especially for women with breasts as ample as hers, and two, because she'd fantasized about this moment. The heat and sound of his breath stirred a deep ache in her core, and she leaned back against him, arching her spine.

He squeezed her breasts, his fingers denting her flesh and making her ache there, too. "Careful of your tattoo," he said, his voice low. "It's probably still a little tender, huh?"

"A little," she breathed, not moving as he circled her nipples with his fingertips, rubbing and then pinching lightly in a way that seemed certain to drive her absolutely crazy. "But I don't mind."

"All the same…" He slid one hand lower, over her belly and beneath her dress, which had pooled around her hips, "we should make a point not to irritate it."

Her head swam as he slipped his fingers into the waistband of her panties and found her clit. Instead of replying, she bit her lip and nodded.

She was already wet – had been from the moment he'd unzipped her dress. He worked his fingertips against the aching bud of her clit, so close to the moisture she could feel on her folds below, dampening her panties. Memories of the night before, in her kitchen, swirled through her mind, but recollections of before she'd left for New York were more powerful. The walls of her pussy shrank at the remembered feel of his hard cock inside her, his shaft stretching her softer flesh.

When he pulled his hand from her panties, her clit throbbed in protest. She'd been close – so close that little tremors were still racing through her core, the almost-bliss fading slowly.

"Come here."

She did, and helped him shimmy what little clothes she'd been wearing off. The lace panties – she'd chosen those especially for this night, too – were the last to go. He paused for a moment, his gaze heavy on the tender area between her thighs, before slipping them off of her.

With nothing on, the air seemed cool against her folds and the hot flesh above. She still ached everywhere he'd touched her – her breasts, her clit – and where she'd imagined him, far inside her core. When he gathered her up and lowered his head to her chest, she gasped as his breath hit her nipples, streaming over their stiff peaks.

He closed his lips around one and drew it past his teeth, simultaneously pressing a hand against the small of her back. The pressure and pull of his mouth against her breast sent a shiver down her spine and another shrinking contraction through her core. He was still dressed, but his erection pressed against her thigh, stiff beneath his jeans.

Visions of slipping those jeans off of him raced through her head, but what he was doing felt so good that she gripped his shoulders instead, letting her nails bite into his muscle. When he raised his head to press a kiss against her lips, she lowered her hands into his lap and undid the fly of his jeans, her heart beating a little faster as the soft, metallic noise of the zipper sounded between them.

She pulled and tugged, getting his jeans off of him and sucking in a breath when he took off his shirt, revealing muscle and ink she'd dreamed about during nights spent alone in New York. She let her gaze rush over his torso, following the slashing lines of his body and curving patterns of his tattoos. Her eyes froze on his right side, by the large, looping script that read *Alice*.

There was a new line of script – a smaller one. It hadn't been there before; she'd memorized his tattoos already. Besides, it was obviously fresh – the ink was a stark black, and the letters were a little raised, the skin red around the edges. Her fingers tingled with the urge to reach out and run her hand down his side, to explore the new feature on his skin. But she didn't dare – it was clearly still healing.

When Jed wrapped his arms around her, reclined on the bed and eased her on top of him, everything else – even his new tattoo – faded from her mind. Straddling his hips, with a knee on either side of him, her pussy was pressed firmly against the hard shaft of his dick.

"Thought this would be an easy way to make sure we're gentle on your new tattoo." He flexed his hips a little, creating a hint of friction between his erection and her slick folds.

She gasped. Easy on her tattoo, maybe, but not the rest of her – her channel was already drawing a little tighter in anticipation. They'd never made love like this. There were a lot of things they hadn't done, really, but it felt natural to rise a little on her knees, allowing him space to slip his hand between their bodies and guide the tip of his cock to her pussy.

He slid inside her in an easy stroke that made her gasp. His motion was smooth, but days of going without his presence inside her had left her tight and aching. Before she could so much as inhale, he pressed his fingertips to her clit, picking up where he'd left off minutes ago as he rocked into her from below.

She managed to breathe – hard – and rolled her hips too, making an effort to complement his movements as everything inside her drew so taut that it felt like she might shatter into a million little pieces.

She braced herself with her hands on his shoulders before she came, holding him hard as the first wave of her climax rushed through her, all heat and tension. He thrust deep into her, each stroke deliberate as he moaned. The sound was a lot like the ones she was making, only deeper.

Coming with him so hard inside her, thick and unyielding in the center of her tightened core, was a feeling that sent pleasure radiating all the way to the tips of her fingers and curling toes. It was most intense in her middle, where it made her pussy shrink and pulse around the base of his shaft. She moved her hips, pushing back and sending him even deeper as she fought for breath.

His thighs were hard as rocks against hers, as firm as the rest of him as he rocked her, making the bed shake as she balanced on top of him, riding out the tail-end of her climax. By the time the contractions had ebbed and the searing bliss had faded, she was breathless and could feel the heat of a full-body blush warming her from head to toe.

He moved his hand from between her thighs to her hip, gripping her there as he continued to push into her hard enough to make the mattress tremble. The vibrations raced up her spine and through her body, defying her to remain still. Still bracing herself against his chest, she held on a little tighter as he groaned, each stroke so deep-reaching that little tremors raced through her core again, like aftershock.

The position made it easy to watch his face. With his head tipped back against the pillow, his hair was as mussed as relatively short hair could be, dark and a little wild around his temples. His eyes were tightly closed, the lashes black against his skin, and his lips still appeared swollen from when they'd kissed. When her name rushed over them, another one of those small internal shivers struck her, drawing her pussy tight again around his cock.

He was still breathing hard when he stopped, and the sound of his breath reminded her of him saying her name. Hearing that always made her glow a little inside.

The window was glowing too, a faint light illuminating the curtain. It was a pure, soft glow – not streetlight. "It's so late," she said, her gaze lingering where the moonlight shone through the window. The excitement of being tattooed and then sex had kept fatigue at bay, but a sleepy feeling was already creeping through her veins, urging her to curl at Jed's side after she rose and slid off of him.

"We can sleep in," he said, gripping her wrist and interlacing his fingers with hers as she stood beside the bed.

She nodded. "I can help you move tomorrow, if you want. I don't have any shoots booked."

"That'd be great."

He was still hard, his cock flushed and gleaming from what they'd just done. A little thrill went through her as she contemplated the next day. Surely they'd find some time to do more than just move boxes. Would she spend the night there with him in the Allegheny West house? Her toes curled against the carpet at the thought.

Visions of the next day continued to play through her mind as she slipped away into the bathroom to get cleaned up. When she returned, Jed was still lying exactly where she'd left him, his head tipped back a little. The position put his body on an appealing display, and the long line of his fresh ink caught her eye. "Your new tattoo is in Latin, isn't it?" she asked as she sank down onto the edge of the bed, her curiosity rekindled now that her lust had ebbed.

He nodded.

"What does it say?"

"*Durate et vosmet rebus servate secundis*. It means 'carry on and preserve yourselves for better times'. I had Eric tattoo it for me last night, after the shop closed."

"I like it. The meaning, I mean, and it looks good on you, too."

He ran one hand down his side, his fingers passing within a bare inch of the new ink as they skimmed over the larger text that spelled out Alice's name. "I got this tattoo just after Alice and I got married. And this one..." he touched the Latin script that sprawled across his left ribcage, "not long after she died."

Thus passes the glory of the world. The words echoed through Karen's mind as she thought back to her first night with Jed.

His fingers still hovered over the black letters. "But this tattoo is more about my grief than her. I always meant to get another one to honor her. I just – I couldn't bring myself to do it. It seemed so final, like if I put a memorial in my skin, the fact that she was gone would be irreversible. I knew that was true, but I didn't want to see a reminder every time I looked in the mirror."

She nodded as something inside her cracked, aching for him.

"I don't feel that way anymore." He met her eyes, and the intensity in his dark irises made her heart skip a beat. "I feel different about a lot of things, lately."

She nodded again, because her throat felt a little too tight and she didn't know what to say, anyway. "What made you choose those words for your tattoo?"

"I read it somewhere – thought it seemed fitting. Alice would've liked it, I think."

"It came from a book?"

"Virgil. The ancient Roman poet. He wrote the line ages ago. Guess he knew what he was talking about." He touched his side again, letting his fingertips skim the fresh lettering. "Not long ago, his words wouldn't have meant anything to me. They would've seemed like a joke. Now that I can see the wisdom in them … I don't ever want to forget them."

"I think it's a great tattoo," she said, placing one of her hands against his palm and entwining her fingers with his.

He was still meeting her eyes, and the depth of his gaze made her words seem shallow. Her emotions were a whirlwind, though, half-threatening to send a tear or two sliding down her face. The tattoo on Jed's side was evidence of a metamorphosis that pulled hard on her heartstrings when she contemplated it.

"I'm glad you think so," he said. "And Karen…" He gripped her hand, exerting pressure that wasn't quite gentle.

"Yeah?" She was still naked, but his attention never wavered from her eyes. Likewise, she couldn't look away from his, not even to let her gaze wander over his new tattoo again.

"I know what love is," he said. "I know that nobody is promised anything, either. Not even one more day, or one more breath. So I have to tell you now, while I have the chance – I love you."

Her breath froze inside her lungs, then rushed out in a sigh she couldn't contain as his words began to settle in.

"I know I was stubborn at first. I was afraid I was wrong for you, afraid my love would hold you back. I didn't want to hinder you."

"You couldn't have been more wrong. Jed, that's not the case at—"

"I know." He squeezed her hand a little more tightly. "I know that now."

She lost the battle she'd been fighting with the stinging pressure behind her eyes. A tear slipped out, and she wound up smiling anyway. "I love you too." Saying it made her feel unbelievably light, like she might rise up and drift toward the ceiling like a helium balloon.

Jed anchored her with an embrace, pulling her close and holding her tight against his chest. In the shelter of his arms, the night seemed suddenly young again. When he pressed a kiss against her mouth, she yielded to the pressure of his tongue against her lips, closing her eyes against the room's faint moonlit glow.

EPILOGUE

Only the lure of buttercream frosting could induce Karen to put down her camera. That and a little encouragement from Jed. "I'm sure you can afford to stop taking pictures for five minutes," he said, pressing a hand to the small of her back and rubbing lightly.

Five minutes? Who was he kidding? It would only take her three minutes, tops, to eat the piece of cake he'd just handed her.

"Come on," he said, guiding her toward a chair at one of the reception hall tables.

She couldn't resist. Not when he was in his groomsman's tuxedo, looking gorgeous in the flattering cut and with tattoos peeking out at the cuffs. She smiled at him as she sank down onto the seat, carefully laying her camera to rest on the tablecloth.

"Mmm. What is this filling, raspberry ganache?" The creamy mixture ran through the center of her chocolate cake slice like a hot pink ribbon, and its smooth sweetness practically melted against her tongue.

Jed shrugged, his broad shoulders rising and falling beneath his tuxedo jacket. "I don't even know what ganache is, but this is good."

He was halfway done with his cake slice already, which made Karen feel less guilty about devouring hers like a starving person. She'd been so busy taking photos throughout the reception that she hadn't taken the time to do more than try a couple bites of Jed's food. The delicious wedding cake hit the spot exactly.

The DJ changed songs, and Karen's gaze was drawn irresistibly toward the dance floor. "They look so perfect together," she said as Mina and Eric glided across the floor to a slow number, both smiling.

Jed nodded. "You must have a hundred photos of them dancing already. You can finish your—"

He gave up as she seized her camera, stood and captured one more. "Any picture might be *the* picture," she said. "The one I put in the frame I bought them in New York."

She was already reasonably sure she'd captured *the one* during the wedding ceremony, but it wouldn't hurt to take another. And another, and another… This was what she loved doing most – capturing images of a once-in-a-lifetime occasion, knowing the photos would be treasured.

"Okay," she said a minute later, settling back into her chair and taking another bite of the heavenly cake. "I'm done taking photos – until this song is over, anyway."

Jed shook his head, but smiled. "You're hopeless."

When the song ended, Karen prepared to leave her seat and get back to work. Before she could pick up her camera, Mina turned and swept toward her, Eric at her side. She looked incredible in her wedding gown, a long white sheath dress with delicate lace panels at the sides that showed off the elaborate tattoo that spanned her ribcage. Eric had done that tattoo for her – that was how they'd met, how they'd begun to fall in love. Mina couldn't have chosen a more perfect gown.

"Karen!" Mina cried when she reached the table, her cheeks flushed and eyes bright from dancing. "Put your camera down and take a break to dance with Jed!"

"I don't want to miss anything," Karen said, "your wedding day only comes once, and I want to make sure I capture it all."

Mina grinned and reached for Karen's camera.

Karen cradled it against her chest like it was her firstborn child, but Mina scooped it up in a similar fashion – a skill probably honed by having raised her little sister. "Here, I'll take one of you and Jed."

Jed stood, wrapping an arm around Karen's waist so that they were posed, facing Mina.

Karen didn't resist – it would be great to have a photo of her and Jed at the wedding. She smiled, blinking after the flash fired. Mina kept going, snapping another photo, and then another.

"Now one with Jess!" Mina said, still grinning.

A small crowd had formed around the table, composed mostly of Hot Ink staff. Jess was there too, looking beautiful in a pink bridesmaid's dress just like Karen's. "Can Blake be in the picture?" Her teenaged boyfriend stood dutifully at her side, clad in a suit and with his hair slicked back.

"Sure," Mina said, and began snapping away as soon as everyone was in position.

For nearly ten minutes, the camera was passed around, which gave Karen a chance to be in group photos with everyone, and in photos alone with Mina. "Thanks a lot, guys," she said when the impromptu photo session was done. "It'll be great to have wedding photos I'm in, but I need my camera back now – it's time for the bouquet toss."

Jed stepped between Karen and Abby, who held the camera. "I'll take photos of the bouquet toss," he said, plucking the camera from Abby's hands, "that way you can participate, Karen."

"You don't have to do that," she said, a blush heating her cheeks as she imagined herself leaping for the bouquet – and maybe even catching it. She had a distinct height advantage over the other women, after all…

"I insist." He cradled the camera protectively, smiling.

"Okay," she agreed, eager not to argue lest she blush the same color as her dress.

In her high heels, Karen topped six feet. She'd never been more grateful for her height than when she queued up with the other female attendees, watching as Mina turned her back to them and called out. "Ready?"

A chorus of encouragement rose up from the little crowd.

Mina tossed the bouquet in a high arc, sending the be-ribboned cluster of white and pink roses through the air.

The flowers tumbled through space, and Karen's heart skipped a beat as it became clear they were heading right for her, like a romance-seeking missile. She extended an arm and rocked forward onto her toes, praying she wouldn't lose her balance.

The bouquet hit her outstretched hand, and she grasped it, grinning.

As she clutched it to her chest, she was buffeted by congratulations and teasing confessions of jealousy, and then there was nothing to do but make her way back to Jed.

"Knew you'd catch it," he said, setting her camera down on the table. "Even got a photo."

"You know what this means, of course," she said, raising an eyebrow and brandishing the flowers.

"Yeah." He returned her grin and wrapped his arms around her waist, pulling her close in a sudden embrace. "I do. The Allegheny West house is too big for just one person, anyway."

"I practically live there already," she teased.

He met her eyes, his expression suddenly serious. "We'll have to make it official one of these days, but you should know – I won't allow you to take the photos at our wedding. You'll have to hire someone else."

He was smiling again, and it was contagious. "I guess I could live with that."

ABOUT THE AUTHOR

Ranae Rose is a best-selling author of over a dozen contemporary, paranormal and historical romances, all of them delightfully steamy. She lives on the US East Coast with her family, German Shepherd dogs and overflowing bookshelves. She spends most of her time letting her very active imagination run wild, penning her next story.

You can learn more about Ranae and her books at...

www.ranaerose.com

19862945R00085

Made in the USA
Charleston, SC
15 June 2013